For Sandy Barron,
who brought Father Ananda to life

THE GARDEN OF HELL

A FATHER ANANDA MYSTERY

NICK WILGUS

SILKWORM BOOKS

The Garden of Hell: A Father Ananda Mystery
© 2006 by Nick Wilgus

All rights reserved. No part of this publication may be reproduced in any form and by any means, without permission in writing from the publisher.

Quotes from *The Sage's Tao Te Ching: A New Interpretation*
by William Martin (Marlowe & Company, New York, 2000)
used with kind permission of the author.

Also available from Silkworm Books:
Mindfulness and Murder: A Father Ananda Mystery (2003)

ISBN 10: 974-93619-4-6
ISBN 13: 978-974-93619-4-8

First published in 2006 by
Silkworm Books
6 Sukkasem Road, Suthep, Muang,
Chiang Mai 50200, Thailand
E-mail address: info@silkwormbooks.info
Website: http://www.silkwormbooks.info

Typeset by Silk Type in Bembo 10.5 pt.
Printed in Thailand by O. S. Printing House, Bangkok

5 4 3 2 1

CHAPTER ONE

"Growing older either reveals or hides the mystery of existence."
—*The Sage's Tao Te Ching: A New Interpretation, #1*

ONE

We were on our way to Sara Buri and the bus was packed with bodies and luggage—we were like sardines in a tin can, hurtling down a two-lane road in the countryside as if fleeing the scene of some crime. It had been my luck to acquire an aisle seat and to find myself sitting face to face with chickens packed in a small wooden cage—a tin can within a tin can, as it were—that was held by an elderly man standing in the aisle beside me who grinned at me with generous lips and what few teeth he still had left.

My traveling companion was a thirteen-year-old novice monk named Jak, who was enjoying the long bus ride far more than I was. We were both dressed in orange robes. He was quite unconsciously reminding me that my own youth had fled long ago, that one did not get to be a Buddhist monk on the other side of fifty without losing some enthusiasm for such things as upcountry bus rides and visits to amusement parks.

That was our destination: Sara Buri Province's famous "Garden of Hell," located on the grounds of a large temple complex called Wat Yai in a provincial backwater a few hours outside Bangkok. As far as amusement parks were concerned, it promised to be slightly different than Disneyland, devoted as it was to Buddhist concepts of hell and demons and whatnot.

I would have preferred just about anything else. I would have even agreed to climbing all the steps at the Temple of Dawn on the banks of the Chao Phraya River in Bangkok. But I had not been given a choice. I had been asked by a representative of the Maha Thera Samakhom—the Buddhist authorities—to "visit" Wat Yai and see what was going on there. More specifically, I was to find out why a nun there had recently committed suicide by throwing herself into the Garden of Hell's crocodile pit, allowing herself to be eaten alive.

My novice companion did not know this, of course. He thought we were on a well-deserved break from Bangkok. I had hopes that the mystery would easily resolve itself and that we would return, he none the wiser, me glad of the fresh air, the peace and quiet.

I hadn't told him that I had been thinking about asking for a transfer to a monastery such as Wat Yai, a place where there would be time for real contemplation and dharma practice, practice of the Lord Buddha's teachings, where the constant noise and busy-ness of life in a major city would come to a screeching halt. Jak would be heartbroken if he knew, since Wat Mahanat, our temple in Bangkok, was his home, at least as much a home as anything could be for an orphan whose parents were both dead. He would not want to leave it—his friends, the fruit vendor who always gave him a free banana when he was hungry, the monks who liked to play cards when they thought no one was watching, the kids who played football in the parking lot in the evenings. He had settled down there, had put down roots, had finally found a place to hang his hat and call his own, had recently become a novice, which gave him deeper roots into our community. No, he would not be in any hurry to leave.

Yet I kept having the strange thought that I should pack a small bag, grab a mosquito net and a walking umbrella, and set off for the forests and jungles as other Thai monks had famously done in the past. I wanted silence, less distraction, less worry, less headache. I was exhausted from meditation classes with junkies who were trying to go cold turkey. I was wearied by Bangkok, the poverty and suffering I saw around me, the lives lived at the margins, lives that consisted of digging through rubbish looking for food, of desperate men and women begging at temples for something to put into their children's bellies, of children showing up on our doorstep with nowhere else to go, hoping that we would take them in as part of our homeless youth program—which was itself already packed with more kids than we could reasonably care for.

I had other reasons for wanting a change that I could not bring myself to discuss with Novice Jak. At least not yet. I glanced in his direction and frowned.

TWO

"Father Ananda, is it true there are guardians in hell who will torture you until you take your next rebirth?" Jak asked. "If that's true, why wouldn't you just take your next rebirth right away? Why wait? Do the guardians have the power to stop you from taking rebirth? I mean, you know, it's really bothering me."

Jak's young, handsome face was screwed up in consternation. He was a thirteen-year-old novice desperate to solve one of life's great mysteries.

"I wouldn't take all of that stuff too seriously," I said. "If you try to do your best, you won't have to worry about hell."

"You don't believe in it?"

"Hell is other people," I said, rattling off one of my favorite quotes. Given that he was an orphan with a leg crippled by polio, and thus was subject to pity and constant stares, he would soon realize the truth of that for himself, if he hadn't already.

"Other people?" he asked.

That was a conversation for which he was not yet ready.

"Don't worry about it," I said. "Hell is for bad people—really bad people. Murderers and rapists and people like that. Not novices who sneak late evening snacks when they think no one knows what they're doing."

"I never do that!" he exclaimed, outraged.

"Don't make it worse by lying."

"Pho!"

Dad!

"And I'm not your dad," I added. "You have to get out of the habit of calling me that. What will the lay people think?"

"Oh please. So you don't believe in hell, Pho?"

"I do," I said. "But we suffer enough in this world without having to worry about some other world where we will continue to suffer. If my karma leads me there, then so be it. I'd rather spend my time trying to develop good karma by making merit in this life. That's what you should be worried about. This life is an opportunity to make sure your next rebirth will be a good one. Don't waste your time worrying about things you can't control."

He did not seem satisfied with this answer.

I reminded myself that he was just thirteen, wasn't the first to ponder such questions, neither would he be the last. I had believed all sorts of things when I was his age, many of which I had since abandoned. I no longer had nightmares about hungry ghosts with tiny little mouths who wanted to suck the life out of my body. I no longer believed that wearing Buddhist amulets could protect me from harm. And I was quite sure that there was more to making merit than offering money to a temple. If one's bad behavior did not change, what was the point of trying to "buy off" the inevitable consequences of that behavior, of that bad karma? You could not buy your way to peace of mind.

"We have to be involved with the way things are, here and now," I reminded Jak, taking a page from the great Thai monk

Buddhadasa Bhikku. "We have no way of knowing what's going to happen to us after we die, so there's no point in wasting too much thought on the matter. Just try to develop as much good karma as you can."

He rolled his eyes and turned to look out the window at the passing rice fields, probably not in the mood to hear another sermon from me. Who could blame him?

THREE

At noon, we pulled up at the Sara Buri bus station. By 1 p.m., we were walking through the gates of Wat Yai with a group of other Bangkok tourists. We were met in the parking lot by a monk named Pandito, our Garden of Hell tour guide. Novice Jak purchased tickets at the booth, his orange robes swaying with the hitch in his step courtesy of the polio—it was not as bad as what some had suffered at the hands of that disease, but quite noticeable nonetheless. I saw other eyes looking at him, knew their stares made him uncomfortable, that he put on a brave face and tried to ignore them, had yet to achieve any sort of holy indifference to the matter. In time, I hoped he would.

"Are we ready?" Brother Pandito called out, gathering us around like chicks under his knowing wings. He was a big sort of man with a weather-beaten face who seemed to highly enjoy his position as our leader and initiator into the mysteries of the Garden of Hell.

Jak and I had our monk's bags slung over our shoulders and were ready for just about anything. This being November, the end of the rainy season, the air was cooler, the sun overhead not quite so hot. It was perfect weather for visiting outdoor gardens and such.

"Are we ready?" Pandito asked again. "Water can be purchased later—no need to carry it, if you don't want to. The tour will only take about thirty minutes, unless you wish to linger."

Several of the pilgrims had already purchased water and were now clutching their bottles like talismans. The smarter tourists had brought umbrellas. Hats could be rented, if one so wished.

Pandito came over to where Jak and I stood. He gave me a long, curious look. "Aren't you that Father Ananda? The one who was in the newspapers a while back?" he asked.

Not this again. I nodded, steeling myself for . . . whatever.

"Folks, it's Father Ananda!" Pandito called out happily. I could hear my name being whispered behind my back as I suddenly became the center of attention. "The one who solved those murders at Wat Mahanat," Pandito added helpfully. "It was in all the papers and on television. Such a pleasure to have you with us today, Father Ananda—no one said we were going to have a celebrity with us!"

I waited for this embarrassing moment to pass. My novice grinned at me, knowing how uncomfortable the fuss made me, how annoyed I had become with it.

Last year I had solved a series of murders at our monastery in Bangkok, which the newspapers and television stations had played up to no end. I had once been a police officer, before taking the robes of a Buddhist monk, and despite my somewhat rusty skills, I had managed to catch a killer. Thanks to that, I had gone from being an obscure monk to a curious sort of celebrity. Now I couldn't go anywhere, even on my morning alms rounds, without someone or other staring at me or whispering my name or giggling when I walked by. At first it had been interesting, even rather amusing. Now it was annoying, a constant test of patience and good will. There were worse problems, though, weren't there?

"Are we ready, folks? Father Ananda, you set?"

Trying not to grimace at being singled out in this fashion, I nodded. Jak took my hand, smiling with anticipation, eager to get on with it.

Brother Pandito led us through the gates and into the Garden of Hell.

The entrance was a long, tunnel-like structure made of intertwined trees, two straight rows, one on either side, the path going through the midst of them. Hanging from the tree boughs were live tree snakes, green in color. The sight of them curled around branches, poking heads and tongues out from behind leaves, was highly disturbing.

"The snakes are perfectly harmless," Pandito said, as we bent our heads low and prayed he was telling the truth. "They are golden tree snakes, rather inactive during the day, and they won't mess with you if you don't mess with them. Unless, of course, you're a bird or a rat or something, and then you'd better watch your step."

This attempt at humor fell flat.

The thought that one of these snakes could fall off a tree limb and land on the top of my bald head produced a distinct bit of revulsion. I was glad to see that the others were just as unnerved as I was. Even Jak was bending low to the ground and hurrying along, although he was flashing me brilliant smiles full of large teeth as if this were just the sort of thing that made teenage boys wild with excitement. Which, of course, it was.

On the ground among the two rows of trees were statues of wild animals—a tiger crouching behind a tree, a vulture pecking at a human corpse, a bear with blood on its snout—each looking rather more plastic than terrifying.

At the end of this path was a small bridge crossing a stream. The bridge was composed of what appeared to be plastic human skulls, which we had to walk over. This was somewhat problematic: touching the head of another with one's foot was about as insulting as it got. To walk across a bridge of skulls? Our party stared at this apparition with a bit of hesitation. Then a brave soul ventured across, triggering some sort of hidden recording that offered a chorus of moans, groans, and the occasional scream. We laughed at this, but the way one laughs on a dark night while trying to appear braver than one really feels. If the intention of this entrance was to put us in a hesitant, uncertain state of mind—to soften us up for the real thing—it was certainly succeeding.

While Jak was enjoying it, I was already wondering when the tour would be finished and how the monks at Wat Yai would take to my poking around and asking questions about their recently deceased nun.

After crossing the "bridge," we found ourselves at the first stop, the "Garden of Lust" exhibit. This consisted of a towering, cactus-like tree with numerous thorns running up its base and scattered along its few large branches. Scrambling up this tree were naked men, Pandito explained, trying to get to their naked mistresses, way up on the top. But the higher the men climbed, the more bloodied and torn their bodies became, until at last they were attacked at the top by giant birds that hurled them down to the ground where they were set upon by the guardians of hell, who hacked at them with knives and swords until they picked themselves up again and made another futile attempt to scale the tree.

"In hell," Pandito said loudly, standing in our midst and looking up the length of the tree with the rest of us, "men who had mistresses will be tormented by having to climb a tree such as this. Their bodies will be ripped open by the thorns as they climb up. They will see their mistresses up at the top, but will never be able to reach them. They will be on fire with lust and desire, but it will never be satisfied. Before they get to the top, one of the birds of hell will attack them and throw them down, where they will be further punished by the guardians of hell. They will have to endure this torment for hundreds of years, day after day, week after week, with no food, no water, no assistance of any kind, until their lusts and desires are utterly exhausted."

We were given an appropriate amount of time to gawk at this strange tree with its lurid women at the top, upon whom some unknown artist had lavished a great deal of attention.

We moved on.

On the long, forested curve leading from the first main exhibit to the second, to the left side of the path, was a very sturdy fence, with small walkways and platforms. We gravitated toward these, wondering what they might offer a view of. We were rewarded with the sight of crocodiles—lots of crocodiles. A sort of river had been made—the concrete bottom was clearly visible, now overgrown with vegetation and water plants. Swimming lazily through this river were crocodiles, some very large. Across the river, on the far side, in sandy areas between the trees, numerous crocodiles were resting, some with their mouths open. Because of the afternoon heat, most were immobile.

Brother Pandito assured us that feeding time provided an excellent opportunity to see these fellows in action.

I could not help but immediately think of the nun who had chosen to commit suicide by jumping the enclosure's fence and letting herself be eaten alive. There could hardly be a more gruesome way to die. To my mind, it seemed calculated, as if the young woman had been trying to make some sort of statement. Had she?

The drop from the fence where we stood to the ground below was about ten feet. The fence itself was only waist high, planted at the top of a concrete barrier that went all the way down and which formed this side of the enclosure's waterway. Had she jumped, she would have first landed in the water.

Jak loved the sight of the crocodiles and was in no hurry to move on. He could not get enough of watching them and pointed out the particularly large ones. He did not look very monk-like, craning his neck over the fence, trying to get a better view, flashing me excited looks. I stood beside him at the fence, unsettled by how large some of the crocodiles were, wondering if there were any way for them to get out.

I tried to imagine a nun standing in the same place, climbing over the fence and jumping down into the enclosure, and the more I thought about it and tried to picture it in my mind, the more implausible it seemed. There were many ways to commit suicide, but to do it in that fashion would require that the victim was seriously off her rocker. From what I had been told thus far, this was not the case. The nun in question was well regarded and had displayed no signs of mental illness or instability, not even a hint that she might have been feeling suicidal.

After we were given sufficient time to gawk at the crocodiles, Pandito had us on the move again.

Our next stop was the "Garden of Falsehoods." Several naked women were in various prone positions in this exhibit, most kneeling on the ground and leaning back on their haunches while the guardians of hell grasped their tongues and chopped them off. On the periphery were more naked woman, tongues missing, blood gushing from their mouths, down their plastic fronts and their rather large breasts. While the male guardians of hell wore tied-up sarongs around their hips, the women had no such coverings for their private parts—whoever had created these "scenes" seemed to have taken great delight in showing women on the receiving end of torture, in positions of vulnerability, on their knees, stripped of their clothes, at the mercy of men.

Where was a feminist when you needed one?

Jak stared at this scene with a frown. I put an arm around his shoulders and steered his eyes away from the sight of the women, deeming them rather too explicit for a thirteen-year-old novice.

"Pho!" he exclaimed in annoyance.

I was grateful when the tour moved on to the "Garden of Cruelty." To get there, we again walked along a tree-heavy path, and among the trees we saw peacocks and other large birds, as well as small ponds and streams, many filled with large gold fish—orange carp, mostly—and here and there, a lone exhibit looking most incongruous with the peaceful surroundings. One exhibit was of a woman being choked by one of hell's guardians. Another exhibit was of the Lord Buddha, standing in the "Thursday" position—holding out one hand, palm facing outward, in the "stop fighting" gesture. Yet another exhibit was of a man in the jaws of a giant cobra being eaten alive.

As we wound our way along the path it took a sharp turn, offering a nice view of a clearing and a single tree—with a rather large tiger sitting beneath it. This tiger was not made of plastic. And unlike the crocodiles, this fellow was not fenced in. Coming upon him so suddenly, as we had, was rather unnerving.

Excited voices quieted, almost instantly. The leader of our group stopped, as did we all. When the tiger got up, as if to lunge in our direction, more than a few of us screamed. All the animal did was find a different spot to lie down. In our excitement, of course, we did not see the collar around the beast's neck. The collar was attached to a chain that was attached to the base of the tree. From somewhere behind the tree, an old man appeared, carrying a sign indicating that photos could be taken with the tiger for one hundred baht. We waited as various souls took him up on this offer. I tried not to think about the foolishness of putting your arm around the neck of a beast like that just to have a picture taken—or of what would happen if the tiger suddenly became tired of such nonsense and decided to have an arm or leg for lunch.

We moved on. It was impossible not to look over one's shoulder and wonder what would happen if the collar on that animal were to break—it did not look very sturdy and tigers are not small animals by any means.

In the "Garden of Cruelty," we were treated to the sight of all sorts of people being tortured, maimed, and tormented for such things as disrespecting parents, speaking unkindly of others or to others, killing animals, gossiping, selfishness and whatnot. There were people being chopped in half with axes, people being beheaded, people having hands cut off, people being eviscerated by large, terrifying animals. The message seemed to be that cruel people would come to a most cruel end.

It was all getting to be a bit much. I looked at Jak, who was taking this all in with wide, innocent eyes. I wondered how it must look to him. Would such scenes frighten him into good behavior? Was that the point?

The next and fortunately the last main exhibit on the tour was the "Garden of Unfaithfulness," and we were treated to the sight of more naked women, these hanging from a large tree. There were about a dozen in all, tongues protruding from their mouths and eyes bulging out, some with their legs spread, some clutching futilely at the nooses that held them fast, choking them to death, all with large breasts, all of it erotic, cruel, crude.

Pandito told us those who cheated on their partners would be hung from such a tree as this in hell, would be left to hang for an endless number of years, suffering thirst and hunger, suffering from the blazing heat of the sun, tormented by birds and insects who would peck at and eat their flesh, causing excruciating agony, all because of their unfaithfulness to their spouses.

Charming.

I wanted to ask why so many of the mannequins were females when it was obvious that males were the most unfaithful of the human species, especially in our part of the world, but I couldn't bring myself to do so—if only because it might prolong the proceedings.

Novice Jak was finding all of this highly exciting; I tried to share his enthusiasm, or at least do my best not to be a spoilsport, but I was glad when we finally walked out of the gates to the Garden of Hell and left the gruesome displays behind.

FOUR

We presented ourselves to Abbot Uddi, the head of Wat Yai, a rail-thin man with a hard face and unreadable eyes. He was seated in the main *sala* and regarded me most carefully as I approached.

"I was wondering when they would send someone," he said, his old voice throaty and high-pitched.

"Pardon me?" I said.

"Come now, Father Ananda. You know what I mean."

I did. I produced the letter from the Maha Thera Samakhom instructing Abbot Uddi to accommodate me and cooperate fully in my investigation, a letter that gave me, basically, the full run of the place, the authority to look at whatever I deemed necessary—the temple complex, the files, records, computers, documents, even living quarters like *kuti* and dorms.

"There was some concern," I said quietly after he had finished reading the letter, "about a nun."

He nodded, took a deep breath, seemed to be collecting his thoughts. I turned to Jak and asked him if he would mind waiting outside while I talked to the abbot. For this I received a rolling of the eyes to indicate his displeasure.

With Jak gone, the man spoke freely. "Sister Mai—that was a shame. It really was. She was very well regarded."

"Any clue as to why she would commit suicide in that fashion?"

He shrugged.

"Any personal thoughts of your own—anything at all?"

"You'll find out sooner or later," he said, and it seemed he was speaking more to himself than to me. "She was pregnant."

Oh.

"Yes," he nodded his head, "that does make it a little more difficult."

An understatement.

"Thinking around here is that she messed up, got herself pregnant, maybe the shame got to her. We don't have many pregnant nuns in this part of the world, you know."

One would hope not.

"I don't think any woman can get herself pregnant," I said. "If I remember correctly, there has to be a man involved."

He smiled.

"Do you know who that man might have been?" I asked.

He shook his head, then glanced around, as if to take in the entire temple complex with its eighty-odd monks, as if to say it could have been any one of them.

"You don't mind if I poke around a bit?" I asked.

His eyes narrowed. He did mind. "Not at all," he said smoothly.

"Anything you'd like to tell me before I get started?"

He shrugged, made a face. What that was supposed to convey, I wasn't sure.

"Anything else strange going on?" I asked. "Anything I should know about?"

He shook his head but would not let me see his eyes. He was lying, in other words. Was not going to be helpful, was going to make me find out things on my own. Undoubtedly he resented having a monk sent from Bangkok by the Buddhist authorities to poke around in his business.

We parted ways, my back up, my mind filled with the image of that crocodile enclosure—and of a pregnant nun throwing herself into it.

FIVE

Jak and I roamed the grounds, orienting ourselves. A mess of chickens strayed across our path and we skirted them. Monks went about the day's business, sweeping up leaves, going off to Pali lessons. Dogs slept in out of the way places.

Wat Yai was blessed with many wonderful green trees, from towering banana trees to palm trees and coconut trees with huge fronds swaying in the breeze, not to mention the monastery's large bo tree in the center of the *kuti*, or the monk's bungalows. Each monastery had such a tree, the sort under which the Lord Buddha had sat to gain enlightenment about two thousand five hundred years ago.

As we wandered deeper into the complex, it became quiet—blessedly so. The air was clean and good to breathe. A breeze blew across the complex, stirring up leaves and grass, treetops, making a gentle, rustling sound. It was a far cry from the chaos of Bangkok with its ten million teeming souls, frantic traffic, pollution, constant agitation, intense heat.

Wat Yai was a bit more orderly than most temple-monastery-school complexes, as we soon discovered. There were three main sections. The middle section was Wat Yai, which included a small dormitory, a large temple where the monks congregated for morning and evening chants and meditations, a crematorium, a large *sala* for public gatherings and religious teachings, a breakfast hall, a funeral hall. The section to the left was the Garden of Hell with its huge parking lot. In the plot of land to the right was the school that most of the village children attended. Lining the dirt road out front that ran past the Garden, monastery, and school were numerous vendors selling foodstuffs and drinks. Traditional-style houses could be seen in the distance.

In the back of the monastery complex were all the many *kuti*, spread out over many acres of tree-heavy land. At most monasteries, the junior monks—those in the robes less than five years—were paired up so that each *kuti* had two monks. The senior monks had *kuti* to themselves. The remainder of the monks took up lodging in the small dormitory. These were mostly the newer monks, or those taking the robes for a few weeks, or a few months, but not planning to stay, as well as some of the elderly, ailing monks who might need assistance during the night should they become ill.

If a man didn't take the robes for even as little as one single day at some point in his life, he was considered *dip*, or raw—like an unripened fruit. Consequently most young men, before getting married, spent some time as a monk, as a way to earn merit for their mothers, or to expose themselves more fully to the teachings of the Lord Buddha before beginning their adult lives in earnest. From what I had seen during my years as a police officer, the Lord Buddha's teachings did not always sink in. At least not with everyone.

The ranks of junior monks were swelled by a number of boys from poor families, much like my novice. By taking the robes, they were assured of an education. For such boys, the life of a novice monk was a high price to pay for that education, but life had offered no alternatives.

In addition to junior monks and senior monks, there were plenty of *dek wat* to be found at any monastery—temple boys, again from poor families, who, in return for work around the monastery tending to the monks and their needs, received an education, or at the very least, room and board. Most of these *dek wat* were nephews of monks, younger brothers of monks, or distant relatives.

As we walked around, I was struck by the male-ness of it all, as if Buddhism was somehow about men and boys and had nothing to do with women and girls. Ironically, it was mostly women who supported monks, who earned merit by offering food each morning as the monks went on their alms rounds, who supported temple fairs and functions, who were always raising money for one thing or another, who always outnumbered the men when religious instruction was given. Without them, our whole ecclesiastical structure would fall—monks would not be able to go forth into homelessness, and a great many boys would lose out on an opportunity to gain an education. We owed them an enormous debt of gratitude. Yet we would not offer them similar opportunities—we would not allow women to be ordained as monks, even though the Lord Buddha himself had allowed it, and had allowed women to form their own monastic communities. Some people even went so far as to say that women could not achieve enlightenment, though the Lord Buddha had made no such claim. It was, in any case, patently false—many Buddhist saints were female.

SIX

We were soon accosted by a monk who introduced himself as Brother Kusalo—the abbot had sent him, had ordered him to see to our needs, to get a *kuti* prepared for us.

Brother Kusalo was short and thin, and wore black plastic glasses that looked stylish, somehow. He had an altogether handsome appearance and an easy smile.

"Let's get you settled," he said easily. "Can't have the famous Father Ananda wandering about homeless, can we?"

Goodness no.

Kusalo led us through the trees, stopping at a bungalow that looked just like all the other bungalows.

"Close to the main bathroom," he explained, climbing the *kuti's* three wooden steps up to the porch, opening the door, checking it out on our behalf to make sure that no wildlife had decided to take up residence within it while it had sat empty, wildlife that could include pythons, cobras, spiders, wasps, lizards, huge centipedes, scorpions—who could tell? Thailand was, after all, a tropical country.

"Looks good," he said, appearing on the porch, smiling a dazzling smile.

He was obviously the "face" of the monastery, the one sent to greet newcomers, take care of guests. "People persons" were always set aside for such tasks, which could easily make it seem as if all monks were happy-go-lucky, good-looking fellows perfectly at peace with the world—which was decidedly not the case.

"I wonder if I might ask you a question," I said.

He trotted down the steps, shifted his orange robes over his shoulders, adjusted his plastic glasses, nodded an agreeable assent.

"Sister Mai?"

For just a moment, a bit of cloudiness passed over his eyes. For just a moment. "The reverend abbot said you would be asking around," he replied.

"I was wondering if you could tell me what happened?"

"Everyone knows what happened. The woman committed suicide. What is there to talk about?"

"How do you know it was suicide?"

He frowned.

"Isn't it possible," I pressed, "that someone could have pushed her over the fence that surrounds the crocodile enclosure?"

"Who would do such a thing?"

"You would have a better idea than I would."

He pursed his lips. His happy-go-luckiness was gone.

"The police investigated?" I asked.

"Of course."

"Their conclusion?"

"Suicide."

"Did Sister Mai seem like the sort of woman who would commit suicide?"

He shook his head, then said he didn't really know.

"When did it happen?" I asked.

He drew in a breath, frowned, scrunched up his face in concentration. "A few weeks ago." He adjusted his glasses again, nervously it seemed. "She did it at night. Went into the Garden. We found her body in the morning."

"No one heard anything?"

He offered a shrug, nodding his head in the direction of the Garden as if to point out how far away it was, how unlikely that anything could be heard from this distance. The Garden could be invaded by Khmer Rouge soldiers, in other words, and no one would know the difference.

"And that's it?" I pressed. "No note? No warning? She just one day—one night—decides to throw herself into the crocodile enclosure?"

"That's the way it looks."

"Looks are often deceiving," I said.

"True enough," he replied. "But you're not suggesting that one of us threw her over that fence?"

"I'm not suggesting anything. Just considering possibilities."

He gave me a curious sideways glance. "Let me show you where the bathrooms and showers are," he said.

SEVEN

"Pho, why were you asking about that nun?"

We were sitting cross-legged on the porch to our *kuti*, resting our feet. Jak's face had a look of worry to it. I decided to play it straight.

"I was asked to look into it."

"Asked by who, Pho?"

"By the Maha Thera Samakhom."

"Really?"

"Really."

"That's so cool! You're going to figure out what really happened?"

"Perhaps. Perhaps not. It's nothing for you to worry about."

"It'll be just like the last time!"

"With any luck, no, it won't be."

He was referring to our previous misadventure, the one that had made me "famous." He had helped, had almost gotten himself killed because of it. I certainly didn't want a repeat of that.

At that time, he was my *kuti* boy, an errand-running assistant, of sorts. Numerous *dek wat*—temple boys—wound up as *kuti* boys to one monk or another, and the relationship usually had more to do with mentoring and fathering than it did with running errands. Since Jak was an orphan, he had latched onto me for all he was worth, and I did not begrudge him though it had taken me a long while to warm up to him.

This was partly the reason that he still called me *Pho*—father. It was a friendly word, affectionate, steeped with familiarity. I had tried hard to get him out of that habit since he was now a monk himself—or at least a novice monk—but to no avail. I was still his "Pho" and probably always would be.

"So you think someone killed her?" he asked, his eyes bright, his face full of excitement.

"I think that you and I ought to do our afternoon meditation . . . that's what I think."

His face fell. Meditation was not nearly as exciting as talk about a possible murder.

"And after that, I think we should wash up and then join the monks for their evening chants," I added.

"Pho!"

"You know the rules."

"I'm hungry," he said, suddenly dejected.

We could not eat solid food after 12 p.m., so there was nothing to do for it but soldier on, drink water or fruit juice, and wait for the day when one's body got used to this lack of food in the latter part of the day. Mine had done so years ago. Novice Jak's had not. He was not above sneaking whatever food he could find, whenever he could find it. Now that we were at a strange monastery, he did not know the lay of the land well enough to know where food might be found. So he was suffering.

"We'll get some fruit juice later," I said, trying to encourage him. "Now, let's do our meditation."

EIGHT

About halfway into our thirty-minute meditation period, a woman dressed in white robes with a shaved head came walking down the path to our *kuti*.

She was a *mae chi*, obviously—a nun. We did not have female monks, properly speaking, as the lineage had died out centuries ago and the current ecclesiastical authorities were hesitant about reviving it. Other countries had done so, but we had not. Still, there were women who took to the robes, lived in poverty and simplicity, taking the Ten Precepts rather than the layman's Five Precepts, doing their best to live the homeless life as the Lord Buddha had outlined.

The nun waited on the footpath, distracting me, making it impossible for me to meditate. Eventually I got up, gathered my robes together, went down the steps to the *kuti*.

"Reverend Father Ananda," she said, addressing me with a *wai* gesture of respect and the title "reverend father"—an abbot—which I was not. I was only a monk.

She introduced herself as Sister Mettha. "I wonder if I might seek a blessing and a moment of your time," she said. "If I'm intruding, do forgive me—I will go away."

She seemed hesitant, uncomfortably submissive, like a dog begging for a scrap from an opulent table who expected to be beaten for her audacity. She seemed most hesitant to speak to me, but then again, most determined.

"Carry on, Novice Jak," I said, glancing up at him on the porch. "I'll re-join you shortly." In response to this, I received a rolled set of eyes and muttering under his breath. I was going to have to say something about that eye-rolling and muttering—again.

Sister Mettha would not look at me. She was wringing her hands together nervously. She kept glancing over her shoulder as if to see whether anyone was watching.

"What can I do for you, Sister Mettha?" I asked. I wanted to touch her arm in a friendly gesture yet did not do so because monks were never supposed to touch a woman for any reason outside of an emergency.

"I heard that you had come," she said quietly. "I was the one who wrote to the Maha Thera Samakhom, asking them to send someone. I never thought it would be you, your being so famous and all."

I waited for her to continue.

"Did you hear about Sister Mai?" she asked, now looking up at me, a trace of anger on the features of her sun-beaten face.

"I did, yes," I replied.

We stood in awkward silence for long moments.

"She didn't kill herself. I can tell you that much."

"Then what happened?" I asked.

"I don't know." The acknowledgment was simple, direct. "But I knew her well enough to know she wouldn't kill herself, not in that . . . fashion. Not at all, as far as that goes."

"Why do you say that?"

"She had life," the nun replied.

"Excuse me?"

"Life. What's the word? She was passionate about being a nun—about everything. She believed in things, was wholehearted, never did anything halfway. What I mean to say is that you could never tell what would come out of her mouth—she was full of surprises, not shy about expressing her opinions. She was a very intelligent woman. She was never the sort of person I would have thought capable of ending her own life. She seemed much too interested in life to do that."

"What was she passionate about?" I asked, curious.

"Female ordination." She said the words, then sighed, looked heavenwards, issued a small laugh. "They all are—the new ones. The young ones. Female ordination. I keep telling them it will never happen, not in our lifetime, but they don't listen, they don't believe me. They want to be monks, right and proper, not second-class citizens. Sister Mai was passionate about that, attended conferences, was always going on about the unfairness of it. I told her we had to make do with what we had. She said we had to make our needs known, force the hierarchy to stop taking us for granted, stop ignoring us."

"Was she so passionate about the matter that she might have committed suicide out of frustration?"

"Hardly, Father. In fact she was all excited about another conference that was coming up, in Bangkok—she already had her bus ticket. I think her parents had purchased it for her. Taking the easy way out? That wasn't her way. She was a fighter."

"Does the abbot know that you wrote to the Maha Thera Samakhom?"

She shook her head.

"Should we keep it that way?" I asked.

"I would appreciate it.

"And what is it you would like me to do, exactly?"

She raised her face to look at me. There was steeliness and strength in that look. Determination. Long-suffering. A very strong will. "I would like you to find out what really happened to Sister Mai."

"You suspect she was murdered?"

"Oh no," she said. "I know she was."

"How do you know that?"

She did not reply. Instead she reached within one of the pockets to her white robes and produced a note, handing it to me with a grim look on her face.

The note said: *Garden 10 pm*

"What does this mean?" I asked.

"We found that in one of Mai's pockets ... after the ... accident."

"And?"

"I don't want to say too much about it, but ... well ... sometimes notes are passed around between the monks and nuns, setting up meetings and such. It's not the first one I've seen."

"In other words, someone sent her a note the night she died, wanting to meet her in the Garden?"

"It looks that way. Of course, we can't be sure."

"Once she was enticed into the Garden, that someone murdered her?"

She shrugged.

"The police investigated?"

"If you care to call it that."

"You mean, they didn't really try to figure out what had happened?" I asked, perplexed.

"They covered it all up," she said, nodding her head in the direction of the monastery where most of the monks of Wat Yai lived. "'Course, everybody around here knows exactly what happened, but they weren't about to go telling the police the truth."

"Why not?"

"Why do you think?"

A former police officer myself, that was a pertinent question. I had seen far too many "suicides" covered up. I knew only too well what police were capable of, how investigations were handled—or mishandled, to be more to the point. She was saying that something was terribly amiss and that those in charge were determined to keep it that way.

"Do you have any idea who might have wanted to do her harm?" I asked.

She shrugged, shook her head. "I wish I did—I really do, Father. But I just don't know. All I know is that something is not right here—something's going on."

"Like what?"

Again she shrugged, shook her head. She did not know.

Our conversation finished, she walked away, head bowed, as if every footstep was an effort, as if life had offered her burdens she could barely carry.

Frowning, I returned to the porch and sat down next to my novice.

CHAPTER TWO

*"We have more questions than answers
and this is a great delight to us."*
—The Sage's Tao Te Ching: A New Interpretation, #14

ONE

That evening, I walked with Jak through the midst of the *kutis*. Just as the sun went down, a racket went up—cicadas. They began calling out, all at once, rubbing their hind legs together to make their peculiar sound. Joining them were frogs and toads, with their distinctive calls. The evening air was cooler than I was used to. In Bangkok, with its skyscrapers and shophouses and endless freeways and alleyways and boulevards and apartment buildings, all the concrete tended to trap the heat, making the city like a giant oven. But out here, away from all that, there was a breeze blowing across rice fields, the rattling of tree leaves, the song of the cicadas and frogs, the wondrous smell of nature and not much else.

Some of the stars overhead could already be seen, though it was not yet fully dark.

Would I find peace in a place like this if I asked for a transfer? Or was I only fooling myself? A change of scenery wasn't going to change the past, was it? It wasn't going to change who I was, what I would bring with me, what I carried inside. It wasn't going to stop me from brooding on all my personal demons.

Jak and I attended the evening chants with the monks of Wat Yai, retired to our *kuti*, went to bed. It had been a rather long day and I was ready to finally lay my tired body down and rest.

On the following morning, we rose early—the gong was struck at 4 a.m., just as it was at all monasteries—and we went about the day's business. Brother Kusalo took us under his wing for the morning alms-round, allowing us to trail behind him as he left the gates of Wat Yai, begging bowl in hand, heading into the nearby community. Jak and I carried our own bowls and were the object of curious stares and smiles among the Buddhist faithful who offered food, fruit juices, cartons of milk, bags of rice, curries, desserts, all manner of foodstuffs.

We did not speak on this morning ritual as it was a time set aside for contemplation of the four things necessary for the sustaining of life: food, water, shelter, medicine. We offered blessings and chants to those of the faithful who requested them. We helped those who wanted to renew their taking of refuge in the Buddha, dharma and *sangha*—the Triple Gem, as it was known, the Buddha, his teachings, and the community of monks he had founded. Otherwise we walked in complete silence. If someone wanted to offer food, we allowed them to do so.

What a change it was from the chaos and concrete of Bangkok! Dirt roads, the air full of the smell of rice fields and flowers and buffalo dung, farms, farmers, farm animals, with wide open spaces to gaze upon and breezes wafting through the fields and catching at our orange robes. If a motorcycle drove by to disturb the tranquility, it was something to be remarked upon. Rarely had I felt such a wondrous sense of well-being and peacefulness.

We were not begging on this alms round. We were going from door to door, as the Lord Buddha once had, presenting an opportunity to those who wanted to perform an act of charity—they could offer food, or money, or fruit juice, or whatever they pleased, or nothing at all. It was a way for lay Buddhists to make merit and start the day by doing a good deed, but no one was under any obligation to offer anything (and on days when that happened, the monks would simply go home empty-handed, spend the day fasting, and try again the following morning).

Compared to walking the pot-holed streets of Bangkok, this alms round was a pleasure. We were accompanied by three of the *dek wat*, whose faces were solemn though they were not above whispering and giggling among themselves when they thought no one was paying attention to them.

As we went from farm to farm, the food we collected was transferred to the plastic buckets that the boys carried. By the time we returned to the monastery, we would have enough food for the monks and the *dek wat* and anyone else in the vicinity who was hungry and needed a meal.

It became readily apparent that we were not going to collect food as quickly as we did in the big city, and there was a certain amount of work involved in walking from farm to farm, encountering each farm's dogs, carefully watching the dirt road to avoid snakes or anything else that might be creeping or crawling about in the early morning hours. We even paused once to wait for a herd of water buffalo to cross the road in front of us.

TWO

After breakfast, Jak and I walked into the village, which was about a mile away. I needed to see whatever passed for the police department in this small town. I needed to see the man in charge.

That turned out to be Lieutenant Poom. When we arrived at his small office, which was located in a building that also served as the village post office and the village health clinic, Lt Poom was on the phone and we sat outside on a bench waiting for him. Waiting and waiting. About twenty minutes' worth of waiting. Enough time to see that his office was hardly larger than a janitor's closet, housed a desk and a tall filing cabinet, had nails pounded into one wall for the hanging of hats and jackets, and little else. Certainly nothing as fancy as air-conditioning or a secretary.

When he finally hung up the phone and turned to acknowledge us, I managed to mask my irritation, knowing that I had just been put into my place—our pompous little officials are masters at keeping people waiting, at reminding the *hoi-poloi* of their dependence on them, of how we have no choice but to wait while the wheels of their bureaucracy slowly churn.

Lt Poom came to the door. I stood, introduced myself and Novice Jak, and asked if I might have a moment of his time.

"Of course," he said, agreeably, as if he hadn't just insulted me by making me sit outside his office for twenty minutes while he talked to his wife (or minor wife or mistress or best friend or whoever) on the phone.

"What can you tell me about Sister Moi?" I asked.

The pleasantness vanished from his face.

"You investigated her death?" I pressed.

"Her suicide, you mean?"

"Her death," I said.

"Nothing much to investigate. She threw herself into the crocodile pit over at the Garden. What else is there to say about it?"

"Don't you think it's an odd way to take your own life?"

"Not really," he said. "I read about it in the papers once, that a woman did it at the Crocodile Farm in Bangkok. Couple years ago—a hundred tourists looking on, and she climbed over the fence and threw herself in—she was dead before they could get her out. It's not really all that odd."

I'd been to the Crocodile Farm once or twice. It was located in Samut Prakan, a suburb of Bangkok. The story about the woman committing suicide there was news to me, but then again, I never had paid much attention to the newspapers.

"Do you have any reason to believe that someone might have wanted to kill her?"

"What for?" he asked.

"I don't know."

"I don't know, either. It was pretty open and shut, Father Ananda. The abbot was satisfied with the conclusion—that it was suicide—and so was I. There were no suspects, nothing like that. Is there some reason why you're asking about this matter?"

"I was sent by the Maha Thera Samakhom to investigate."

"To investigate?"

"Yes."

"I wish you luck, but there really isn't much to investigate."

"Would it be possible for me to have a look at your file on Sister Moi—your report?"

He turned his head to look into his office, seemed suddenly hesitant.

"I'm afraid my files are confidential," he said quietly, turning back to me. "I'd need to get clearance from higher up."

"Would you?"

"Get clearance?"

"Yes. I can wait."

"Oh no, sorry, I'm afraid it would take awhile. Why don't you come back in a few days?"

"I'd really like to see that file today."

"That's just not possible."

"No one needs to know."

"I just can't help you. Sorry. Now if you'll excuse me. Need to make my rounds."

He closed the office door behind him, locked it, was out the door as though the building was on fire.

I sat down on the bench, put my face in my hands. Jak sat beside me.

"Do me a favor," I said to him. "Must be somebody here with a key to this office—the janitor, maybe, the building supervisor. Go ask if they could unlock the door. Tell them I left my bag in there, just need to get it out."

"But that would be lying!"

"Even so. Do it for me. And when you find someone to unlock the door, keep them occupied for a minute so that I can look through that filing cabinet. Okay?"

He grinned, sensing that mischief was afoot. He shuffled off, eventually returning with a middle-aged woman who was in charge of housekeeping.

"You're that Father Ananda," this woman exclaimed happily. "I knew it—I saw you come in. What brings you to our little village?"

"Just visiting the Garden," I said, for once grateful that my "fame" could be put to good use.

"Everyone visits that place," she said, smiling.

I nodded at the door. "Left my bag in there, some papers and Lt Poom is already gone. Sorry to trouble you."

"It's no trouble at all," she said.

She unlocked the door. No sooner did it swing open than Jak tripped and fell, almost at her feet, howling with (supposed) pain. She immediately bent down to help him, to fuss with his crippled leg, to make sure Little Novice Orphan Boy was all right. He played the ruse for all it was worth.

While that was going on, I hurried into the small office, browsed through the filing cabinet. I had guessed—correctly—that a small-time officer in a small village would not have many case files on hand. He did not. Sister Moi's was right in front. I grabbed it, slipped it beneath my robes, was out of the office in less than ten seconds.

Jak was moaning and carrying on as if his leg had been broken in twelve different places.

I knelt, inspected the "injured" limb, urged him to be quiet, to stop making such a fuss, that it was unbecoming of a novice.

"It looks okay to me," I said, glancing up at the woman.

"Let's just get him to the health clinic to be sure," she said. After all, the health clinic was just ten feet away.

"No, really," I said. "He looks fine. His ankle is just a bit sensitive sometimes—he's always going on about it."

She pursed her lips in motherly concern.

I "helped" Jak to his feet, allowed him to clutch at my arm while he hobbled out the front door.

"You got it?" he whispered, looking up at me and smiling.

"Thanks to you, yes."

THREE

We walked through the village, exchanging pleasantries with the natives, taking in the country simplicity and healthy air. We stopped at a large noodle shop, not because we were hungry but because I wanted to engage in small talk with the villagers while having a quick look at Moi's file.

We were served by a girl who was no more than ten; we ordered two cokes. Many of the twenty-odd tables were occupied, too many for me to look at the file. So instead of reading it, I transferred it to my monk's bag. It would have to wait. I smiled in greeting at a couple of old women sitting at a table nearby.

"You look familiar, Father," one of the women said. She was wearing typical country garb. A loose blouse, a brightly colored sarong around her waist, cheap flip-flops on her dusty feet. Her face was all wrinkles and curves, frizzy hair tied up with a rubber band. "Do I know you?"

"My name is Father Ananda," I said.

Her companion, similarly dressed, smiled widely. "Of course. You were in the newspapers!"

"That's me," I said, trying to take this in graciously, aware now that many eyes had turned in my direction, that ears were listening to this conversation.

"Been to visit the Garden of Hell," I said.

The first old woman laughed. "You and the rest of the world. Folks is coming from all over to look at that thing, would you believe it?"

"There was some trouble there recently, wasn't there?" I said.
"You mean Sister Moi?"
I nodded.
"Oh, a terrible thing. Yes, a terrible, terrible thing. Terrible."
Her companion agreed, a stricken look on the features of her ancient face.
"Did you know Sister Moi?" I asked.
They both nodded. The first lady said Moi was a "good girl."
"Do you know why she might have committed suicide?"
"Oh Father, everybody knows that's not what happened."
"Really?" I played the innocent.
"Don't believe everything they say—that abbot over there and his minions."
Those were pretty strong words. Monks were generally held in high regard. They were rarely referred to as "minions."
"What I mean to say," she went on, lowering her voice, as if we were sharing a delicious conspiracy, "is that the Garden makes a lot of money—they don't want to scare off the tourists with talk about murder. Know what I mean?"
I did indeed.
"So they said it was suicide. Ha! And I'm Miss Thailand."
There were sniggers at this, general amusement at the thought that this old crone could be Miss Thailand.
"So what *did* happen?" I asked, trying to be very gentle and nonchalant about it.
She shrugged. "Don't nobody really know, I suppose. But you'll find few folks who believe Moi did herself in, especially that way. That girl was full of fire, if you know what I mean. She had more energy than a snake's got cunning. She was a smart girl, not like some buffalo sitting around thinking about drinking a bottle of pesticide 'cause her husband ran off with the *mia noi*."
The minor wife.
"Was she from these parts?" I asked.

"'Course she was. Her family lives not a mile from Wat Yai."
"Can you give me directions?"
She could, and she did.

FOUR

"We're going to walk there?" Jak asked.

"Don't see any buses around here, do you?" I replied.

"My leg is killing me, Pho. For real. I twisted it when I fell down. Overdid it, I guess."

I looked down at his crippled leg, suddenly realizing that I had put him through a lot that day—the morning's alms round, the walk back into town, now another mile's walk to visit Sister Moi's family.

"I forgot," I said. "We can go some other time."

"No, it's okay. It'll be all right."

"You need some rest."

"Maybe we could take a taxi?"

That was an idea, but there were no taxis to be seen, only a stand of motorbikes with a few young men milling around. After telling them where we wanted to go, we were charged the princely sum of ten baht each and were on our way. In Bangkok, we had to pay thirty-five baht just to get into a taxi.

I had forgotten that motorbikes and monks don't mix well, not when a monk is wearing what basically amounts to three sheets. The potential for embarrassment is quite significant. With the wind whipping up my legs and around my arms, billowing my robes about, I could only hope that nothing would go flying off into the rice fields.

It was a relief to stop in front of an old farm house on a lonely country road.

"Why don't you wait here?" I suggested to Jak, more a command than a suggestion.

After our two motorcycle taxi drivers agreed to wait as well, I walked alone down the driveway to the house, was quickly greeted by a pack of dogs who looked like they would rather rip my robes to shreds than roll out a welcome mat. I paused a good distance from the house, not really bothered by the dogs, knowing they would raise enough ruckus to bring someone to the front door, which they did. A boy. Looked to be about fifteen. He hurried down the steps, called the dogs off, sent them packing with claps of his hands and angry grunts.

"Reverend Father?" he said, offering a *wai* gesture of greeting.

"I wonder if I might talk to your parents. Are you the family of Sister Moi?"

At the mention of his sister's name, the boy frowned. Saying nothing, he hurried off. The dogs, in his absence, now came round again, sniffing at me, trying to decide if I was friend or foe. The boy returned with a woman who was bent with age and care and too many years bending over in a rice field, planting shoots, harvesting. She offered me a *wai* but said nothing.

"Are you Sister Moi's mother?" I asked.

She nodded.

I introduced myself, explained that I was investigating her daughter's death. This caused the woman's eyes to mist over, her look of interest replaced by a faraway expression, as if searching for something in the distance.

"I would like to ask you a few questions, if I could. Are you up to it? I could return some other day, if that would be more convenient for you."

She did not reply. Instead she went to the steps to the house and sat down, putting her arms on her knees, hanging her head.

"Should I leave?" I asked the boy, glancing up at him.

"No. Just give her a moment. We don't talk much about . . . it."

I walked slowly to the steps and sat down on them myself, next to the woman. Not a very monkish thing to do, but then again I wasn't always very monkish, and concerns about sexual impropriety were way down on my list of things to be concerned about. That's one of the benefits of being more than fifty years old. Sex is no longer that interesting.

"I'm sorry," I said to her quietly. "I know it must be very hard for you."

She started to get up, perhaps sensing it wasn't quite right to be sitting next to a monk, as if we were on an equal basis, as if, out of respect, she wanted to make sure her head was lower than mine. I motioned to her that it was okay, that she did not have to get up, that we could dispense with the formalities and talk like we were just old friends having a small chat.

"Do you want to tell me about it?" I asked.

She looked at me now, at this strange monk from Bangkok prying into her private business. "She didn't kill herself," she said. "I don't know what happened over there, but it wasn't that."

"How do you know?"

"A mother knows."

We regarded each other in silence.

"Do you have any idea what might have happened?" I asked.

She took a deep breath, turned her eyes away, as if searching in the distance for something. "All kinds of stuff goes on over there. I told my daughter to go to Bangkok if she wanted to be a nun, not over there. Don't trust those people."

"Why not?"

"I don't know. They make a lot of money with that Garden, and money always causes trouble. And the abbot . . . he's . . . well, you know, as they say, connected. His brother's a big to-do in this province, is what I'm saying."

"Mafia?"

"But you didn't hear that from me."

"Anything suspicious been going on over there?"

"Some talk, yes. I've heard things."

"What things?"

"Moi would hint about things, would never really come out and say it, so I don't know. Mostly the nuns over there take care of those foreign children, and she often used to wonder what exactly was going on with them."

"How do you mean?"

"Well, she said the children would come at night, would be packed into the dorm. The nuns would see to their needs, but the children were always coming and going—no sooner than they settled down for a few days than they were sent off again, and new kids showed up. Said she asked the abbot about it and was told to mind her own business."

"You think the monastery is involved in child trafficking?"

She gave me a blank stare. She obviously did not know what child trafficking was.

"That's when children are taken from their parents and sold off to adoption agencies, or made to work as maids, or sent off to brothels in China or Japan . . ."

She frowned, looking puzzled, as if this thought—this activity—was just about the strangest thing one could ever hear. "You must be joking," she said.

"Thailand is a hub in the child trafficking business," I pointed out. "Women are trafficked too."

It took her a while to sort this out in her mind. A simple country woman, she probably didn't know half the things that our criminal element got up to, and would be horrified if she did.

"Trafficking those children?" she asked, eventually. "What for?"

"Mostly they are used as cheap maids or sold to brothels."

"Brothels?"

I nodded.

"What for?"

I didn't want to have to spell it out too clearly, so I waited for it to sink in. "Chinese men," I said, "have the belief that sex with a virgin will cure them of sexually transmitted diseases like AIDS—so young girls are in special demand."

"What kind of nonsense is that?"

I shrugged. I was the conveyer of bad news, and it made no more sense to me than it did to her.

"Well, maybe that's what it was," she said quietly. "Moi said those kids were constantly coming and going. In 'batches,' she said. One batch in, one batch out. Kids from Cambodia, mostly. Some from Burma, Laos. All of them poor and ragged-looking. The nuns were supposed to help clean them up, get some fresh clothes for them, fill their bellies. Moi loved that sort of work, loved those kids, loved 'shining them up,' as she put it, shining them up like you'd shine up an old coin or an old shoe. But then, just as soon as she'd start getting attached to them, off they went and another batch came in."

"The abbot must have offered some sort of reason," I pointed out.

"Word is, the kids are being sent home, or sent to refugee camps. The nuns clean them up, as it were, in preparation. But nobody knows what becomes of them after they leave. And since they're always coming and going at nighttime in all those vans, I guess it just seems odd to us. You know? Like maybe they're doing something wrong, something they don't want people to know about. I mean, why would you wake those kids at three in the morning to send them off to wherever it is they're going? Those kids need their sleep. Why can't it be done in the daytime like normal folks do things?"

"Do you think Moi was suspicious about this—and maybe the abbot didn't like it? Maybe they wanted her silenced?"

She sighed heavily. "I don't know what to think, Father. I really don't. After Moi's ... death ... the abbot came 'round, gave us one hundred thousand baht. Just like that. To help us with our loss, is what he said. But I had the feeling he wanted us to be quiet about it, to just accept it and move on. So that's what we've been trying to do. Of course, I have my questions and my doubts, but I'm just a farm woman and there isn't anything I can do. So we just took the money and let it go, you know? What else could we do?"

"Did he tell you not to speak about it?"

"Not in so many words. But he said if any reporters ever came along, trying to 'stir up trouble' about it, that we was to send them over to Wat Yai and let him deal with it. Told us it was for our own protection, that those reporters would print the most awful things about us if they decided they didn't like us."

Which was probably true, I thought.

Now it was time for the hard part. "Your daughter was . . . pregnant."

Her eyes shot a glance at me, then away, back to the ground.

"Did you know that?" I asked.

"Not till she died," the woman replied. She put her face in her hands. She was clearly distressed.

I waited, wanted to give her time to deal with this particular demon.

"Do you have any idea who the father might have been?"

"The father?" She seemed incredulous, as if the thought had never occurred to her. "I didn't even know she was pregnant. How am I supposed to know who the father was?"

"I was only wondering."

"My daughter wasn't that way."

"What way?"

"The type to fool around. With men. She wanted to be a nun. As far back as I can remember, she's wanted to be a nun. That was all. She never had any doubt about it. And she didn't go off and become a nun just to fool around with a man. She took the homeless life very seriously."

"Did she have any enemies that you know of?"

"Enemies? She was a nun! What kind of enemies could she have?"

"Is there anything you can think of that might help me figure out what happened to your daughter?" I asked. "Who would want to do such a thing to her?"

"I don't know," she confessed. "I just don't know, Father. Don't suppose I ever will. I told her to go to Bangkok, but she was so headstrong—always was, that girl."

I thanked her for talking to me, asked her to let me know if she thought of anything else. I told her that I would be staying at Wat Yai for a few days and that she was welcome to come and talk to me any time she wanted to.

As I walked away, I could hear her crying softly.

FIVE

Abbot Uddi's office had many more filing cabinets than Lt Poom's, as I discovered when I asked Brother Kusalo whether I might have a look at the files on the monks at Wat Yai.

"The abbot's not going to like it," Kusalo said, offering a smile as if to suggest he did not always follow the abbot's orders.

I gave him a long look, knowing that I needed this man's help. More specifically, I needed his confidence. I needed an insider at Wat Yai to help me figure out what was going on. Yet I did not want to share any of the information I had learned thus far. Even so, I had to—I needed this man to trust me, to help me.

I took the note that had been found in Moi's robes, spread it out on the man's desk. I wanted to compare this note against the handwriting in the files for the monks. I explained this to him.

"You think whoever wrote this note might have killed her?"

"Perhaps."

"Well. Let's get started."

We decided that I would start at the end of the files, that he would start at the beginning, and we would work our respective ways to the middle.

One at a time, we spread out the files, compared the handwriting. We worked steadily for perhaps an hour, with no luck. Jak sat in the waiting room, resting his leg, looking bored, which he no doubt was.

I glanced through each of the files to see if something relevant might turn up. I was hoping to find at least a few suspects to look into. But the files were clean. After two hours we had very nearly reached the end and I found no obvious handwriting matches.

So much for that clue.

SIX

"Where's the cell phone?" I asked Jak after we had returned to our *kuti* for a bit of rest.

"In my bag," he said, getting it for me then pronouncing that it was dead, that the battery had died out.

"Well, that's not much help," I said, frowning.

"They *can* be recharged, you know," he said, rolling his eyes. All of us adults were, of course, complete idiots. And when it came to all this new-fangled technology, that was pretty much the truth.

"How long will that take?" I asked.

"An hour."

"But I want to make a call right now."

"And you will, Pho. Give me a minute. Sheesh!"

He found an adapter, plugged it in. The phone lit up. "Make your call," he said, handing the thing to me.

I dialed Wat Mahanat, our monastery in Bangkok. Kittisaro, the abbot's secretary, answered, as I knew he would.

"I need your help," I said straight off. "Can you get on the Internet and do a search for me?"

"Of course I can. And hello to you, Father Ananda. We're fine, thanks for asking. So nice of you to be concerned about us."

"This is important."

"So is courtesy."

"Okay. How are you, Kittisaro? How're your hemorrhoids these days?"

"I don't have hemorrhoids."

"You will if you don't stop fooling around and listen to me. This phone's going to die any second."

"No it isn't, Pho," Jak called. "When it's plugged in, you can talk as long as you like. Even I know that."

"Search for what?" Kittisaro asked. "You guys having fun at the Garden of Hell?"

"Murderously so," I said. "I want to search the Internet for anything you can find on the Garden, Wat Yai, the abbot, mafia connections, child trafficking, a repatriation program, something to do with kids."

"Is that all? We could do a search on how to solve world hunger too, if you'd like."

"That's all."

"Child trafficking in general . . . or what?"

"Child trafficking as in why are so many Cambodian kids being processed through Wat Yai—where are they from, where are they going?"

"You think Wat Yai is part of a trafficking ring?"

"I think it might be one of the stops, yes."

"Well, they don't usually post information like that on the Internet, but I'll see what I can find."

"You can look in newspaper archives, can't you?"

"This is the twenty-first century, Ananda. We stopped using microfilm ages ago."

"What is microfilm?"

"Never mind. I'll get right on it. I'll let you know. And Ananda?"

"Yes."

"You got another love letter. Would you like me to read it to you?"

"What's the point?"

"It's colorful. You sure?"

"No. I could care less."

"It's making the abbot even more nervous than he usually is."

"Doesn't take much."

He agreed that no, it did not take much to get the abbot upset.

"Just put it with the others," I said.

"Okay. But watch your back. You're not a spring chicken anymore and you've made enemies with some of the wrong people."

"Gotta go."

I hung up the phone, stared at Jak, who was lying flat on his back, which he usually did when his leg really *was* hurting. I hadn't told him about the postcards—the "love letters" as Kittisaro and I called them. Hadn't been able to bring myself to do so. It was those love letters that had got me to thinking about leaving Wat Mahanat, about packing a mosquito net and heading for the forests, not only for my own safety but Jak's too. As long as I remained at Wat Mahanat, we were both at risk, as our postcard correspondent continued to point out.

"You okay?" I asked, frowning at him.

"Just a little tired," he said.

I went out on the small porch, sat down on the steps, looked at the file for Sister Moi, wondering how I was going to be able to get it back to Lt Poom without his noticing. Aside from sliding it under the door, I didn't have many options.

The file was woefully inadequate. There were pictures of the scene, of a woman in white, albeit muddied, robes lying on the sandy banks of the crocodile enclosure, then another set of pictures of her body inside the death room being prepared for the funeral. Her robes were stained with blotches of her own blood. The right shoulder had been attacked, a sizeable chunk removed. One foot was missing. The face was messed up by bite marks. Little red flecks could be seen here and there on her face—blood? Burst blood vessels? It was hard to tell.

Altogether it was rather gruesome.

Included with the report was a piece of orange cloth in a plastic evidence bag, obviously something found at the scene that Lt Poom had collected and bagged. The color was unmistakably monkish: it was obviously a piece of a monk's robe. Had our killer, in the struggle to push Sister Moi over the fence, torn his robes?

The report itself told me no more than I already knew, except for one small detail: the body had been found by Brother Pabhassaro, the Garden's chief maintenance man.

Brother Pabhassaro and I needed to have a conversation.

SEVEN

That evening I heard dogs barking at just after midnight. I got up from my mat, went out onto the porch of the *kuti*, and listened to the ruckus.

Dogs and temples went hand in hand, of course. Temples were a convenient place to drop off unwanted pets, thus each temple had its share of canine hangers-on. They made a lot of noise at the 4 a.m. wake-up gong, but were usually quiet the rest of the time—quiet, unless something or other was going on.

Aside from me, I could see no one else. The barking seemed to be coming from far away, over in the direction of the Garden. I thought about the Garden and involuntarily shivered. All those animals—crocodiles and snakes and who knew what else—and exhibits, all the gore and gruesomeness of it all, all of it so close at hand. It made me uncomfortable. How could these monks live so close to such a thing and not be affected, not worry about the potential consequences? Or were they hardened to the Garden's dubious charms?

The dogs barked. I listened. Eventually they quieted.

Alone, on my porch, the stars a brilliant sight overhead, the trees rustling every now and then. I felt a sort of dread settling upon me, as if the darkness and shadows around my *kuti* hid deadly secrets, as if Jak and I might be in danger here in this seemingly quiet place.

Eventually I went to bed.

CHAPTER THREE

"Trying to make a perfect life is a path of great sorrow."
—*The Sage's Tao Te Ching: A New Interpretation, #45*

ONE

On the following morning, it quickly became obvious that something unusual was going on. The gong was struck at 4 a.m., as usual. The dogs raised a ruckus, as usual. Monks dressed in sarongs with towels over their shoulders headed to bathrooms and showers to do their morning business and prepare for the day ahead—as usual. But the monks were going about their business in a hurry, as if desperate to get dressed and . . . what?

Jak and I brushed teeth, splashed cold water over bald heads, rubbed sleep out of our eyes. I don't think he noticed the changed mood, the tenseness. Like most teenagers, he found it hard simply to wake up and get going.

We went back to our *kuti*, got our robes on. Kusalo came down the path, called my name. I poked my head out the *kuti* door.

"I think you should come," he said.

"What is it?"

"Just come," he said. He motioned with his hand.

Jak and I followed. Kusalo led us through the temple complex, out to the parking lot, over to the Garden of Hell. We made the treacherous trip through the trees with their confounded snakes—my skin crawled at the thought of how they were sleeping in the branches above our heads—over the skull bridge, to the Garden of Unfaithfulness exhibit.

Several monks had already gathered at the exhibit, and were gawking at the tree with its lurid women hanging from concrete branches.

Among them, on this particular morning, was a monk.

"That's Brother Pandito," Kusalo said, his voice a mixture of dread and excitement. "He must have committed suicide!" He looked at me, his eyes all but unreadable in the darkness and shadow.

Two suicides? That was about as likely as the Buddha owning a hotel in Las Vegas.

TWO

Abbot Uddi was summoned. He spent a lot of time staring up at Brother Pandito, who was outlined in the glare of various torches. The abbot turned around and told the monks to go back about their business. Something about his voice kept them from disagreeing. Meekly, they lowered their gazes from the vulgar display, hurried off.

In the silence following their departure, the abbot turned to look at me. He was carrying a torch and trained its beam at my face.

"That includes you," he said.

"I would rather stay and figure out what's going on here—that's why I was sent."

"It's obvious, isn't it?" he asked.

"Suicide?"

He nodded.

"No," I said. "It's not obvious at all."

"You think someone strung him up here? People do kill themselves, you know. Not everything has to be murder."

"May I?" I asked, motioning for the torch light.

He handed it to me. I trained the beam on Brother Pandito, standing just below him now, using the light to outline his body, his bare chest, the sarong tied about his waist, the rope tied about his neck. The rope had formed a V-shaped pattern, curving around the neck, disappearing on both sides underneath his ears. There were strange markings on his neck as well—a series of blotches in a straight line in a decidedly non-natural pattern, as if they had been made by a chain. I put a hand on the man's belly, checking for temperature. Bodies cool at a certain rate. If the body is warm, then death has occurred within less than three hours. If clammy, from three to twelve hours. If cold, more than twelve hours. This body was clammy. I thought about the dogs barking last night at around midnight, thought it was safe to guess that Pandito had died at about that time.

I gently gave the man's hip a push so that the body would turn around, shining the light on his back, seeing what I expected to see—blotches and bruising. I examined his legs and feet; they were normal. I checked his fingernails carefully for signs of dead skin—many victims scratch or scrape their murderers, leaving traces of skin beneath their fingernails. On the index and middle finger of Pandito's right hand, I saw telltale skin scrapings—someone would be walking around today with a scratch on their body.

There was another odd thing: red flakes, like the ones I had seen in the pictures of Sister Moi. They were on Pandito's face. They looked like tiny chips of dark red paint, a few on each cheek, one on his upper lip.

"Well?" Abbot Uddi demanded.

"Any reason why this man would do this to himself?" I asked. I knew he had not committed suicide but I wanted to play out the scene, see where it led.

"Who knows?" the abbot replied. "Half these monks are fruitcakes who can't get jobs, and the other half are running away from their wives and responsibilities. What do you expect?"

That wasn't really a fair assessment of monastics, but I was not in the mood to take up the matter. "You've called the police?" I asked.

"Of course we have," the abbot replied. "We're not idiots just because we live in the country."

I bit off a sharp reply.

"Get this body down," the abbot ordered. Aside from myself and Jak, only Kusalo, the abbot's assistant, had remained.

"We should leave it up until the police arrive and do their investigation," I pointed out.

"What's to investigate?" the abbot demanded.

"This man did not commit suicide."

The abbot threw a contemptuous look at the body, as if it was a problem he did not want to be responsible for, as if it was just one more thing in a long list of things that were annoying him to no end.

"You wait for the police then," he announced. "I've got better things to do."

He marched off.

"Don't mind him," Kusalo said in his absence. "He gets that way sometimes. Doesn't like people messing up, creating trouble for him."

"Is that what this monk has done? Messed up?"

Kusalo shrugged.

"You knew him, of course?"

"I did," Kusalo agreed.

"What can you tell me about him?"

"What most people will—he is . . . was . . . Sister Moi's brother."

"No kidding." I was flabbergasted. A brother and sister had committed suicide? What were the chances of that?

"Ever since her death," Kusalo said, "he hasn't been himself. I'm not surprised that he did this, actually—if you want to know the truth."

"Why is that?"

"How would you feel if you were living in the same monastery with the man who had raped your sister?"

"Excuse me?"

He adjusted his glasses, knew he had my full attention. "Moi accused Brother Panya of raping her, but Panya was given an alibi by his brother, who is also a monk here—Brother Subha. So nothing could be done about it. It was her word against theirs, the word of a nun against the word of two monks. Pandito was angry about it, of course, but that's how things are sometimes."

"How do you know all this?"

"Sister Moi complained to the abbot that Panya was harassing her. She wanted a stop put to it."

Kusalo, being the abbot's assistant and secretary, was the sort of person who would know most of the abbot's business, who would know about meetings, visits, reports, things usually kept confidential—each monastery had their fair share of such things.

"He was in love with her?" I asked.

"Yes. And eventually he raped her."

"You know this for a fact?"

"I don't know. Nobody does. She told the abbot about it. The abbot didn't really believe her—I couldn't hear everything that was said, the door to his office being shut and all. But I don't think he believed her. And Subha provided an alibi anyway. Moi said it happened on a Wan Phra night."

"A full moon night?"

"Yes. But Panya and Subha always spend their Wan Phra nights at the crematorium—everyone knows that. They've done that ever since they came here three years ago."

Full moons were special days on the Buddhist calendar, and they called for even greater efforts at meditation and the practice of dharma. If Panya and his brother Subha spent their time "at the crematorium" then they were probably meditating on death and dying, a common practice among monks.

"So the abbot thought Sister Moi was lying," I said.

"I suppose. You would have to have known her—she was pretty strong-willed. Insistent about things, always wanted to have her way. The monks didn't like her much—she was always a bit provocative, if you know what I mean."

"I don't think I do."

"A bit too friendly. Flirting, I guess you could say. You never knew what was going on in her mind, what she was really after."

"Oh."

"Several of the monks complained about it. There's nothing wrong with having a few old nuns about the place, but Sister Moi was a distraction, especially since she was always getting into everyone's face, always telling everyone how things ought to be done. She was a pain in the backside, in other words."

"Then she came up pregnant?"

"Yes. I think she was too proud to admit what she'd done, or who she'd done it with, so she lied about it, blamed it on Panya, and maybe in the end she killed herself because she was ashamed—maybe she realized that people were going to find out the truth and she wouldn't be able to talk her way out of it."

I stared again at Pandito's body, my mind filled with confusing thoughts. What was his mother going to feel, now that two of her children had come to a bad end at this monastery? That was a silly question, of course—she was going to be absolutely devastated.

What was going on at this strange temple in the middle of nowhere with its lurid Garden and crocodiles and snakes?

"Doesn't it seem a bit . . . odd?" I asked. "Two deaths? Brother and sister?"

Kusalo readily agreed.

THREE

"Looks like suicide," Lt Poom announced. He plucked one of the tall grasses nearby and chewed on it nervously. In the early morning sunlight, he looked taller and thinner than he had the day before. "Must have come out here last night with the rope and hanged himself. I guess he had his reasons."

He crossed his arms over his chest.

The abbot had returned. He glared at me, as if defying me to say something.

"I beg your pardon?" I said. Until then, I had been standing by quietly, viewing the proceedings with increasing alarm. "I hardly think you can draw any conclusions just yet," I added.

"And why is that?" the abbot asked. There was a sneer to his voice.

"The bruising on the man's back."

"What of it?"

"That's where the blood settled."

The abbot frowned.

"When someone dies, the blood follows the path of gravity," I explained. "Obviously this man died lying on his back, which is where the blood settled. If he had hanged himself, the blood would have settled in his legs and feet. As you can see, that is not the case."

"Doesn't prove anything," the abbot said quietly.

"It proves he didn't hang himself—he didn't lie dead on the ground long enough for his blood to settle in his back and then tie himself up to a tree."

The abbot gave me an unfriendly frown.

"It looks like suicide to me," Abbot Uddi said quietly, as if to see whether I would dare challenge him.

Suicide? It was ridiculous.

"Carry on with your work, officer," the abbot said to Poom. Then he took my arm. "Father Ananda and I need to have ourselves a small talk." He led me away from the crime scene—that was the way I thought of it, a crime scene, a place where something criminal had happened—to a place where we could talk in private.

"I disagree," I said straight away. "This man did not commit suicide."

He gave me a long, searching look. "Do you know how many tourists visit our Garden every year?" he asked.

What did that have to do with anything?

When I didn't answer, he said, "About fifty thousand. Every year. Numbers keep going up. Do you know how much money this community makes from all those visitors—lodgings and accommodations, food, buses, taxis, souvenirs, entrance fees, bottles of water? You see, we don't have the sort of resources you have over there in the big city, Ananda. Lots of the menfolk in this community have lost their jobs. Lots of the kids want to go to university but can't afford it. Now if you go off and tell the press that someone has been murdered here, what will that do to us?"

"But you know he didn't kill himself," I replied, understanding his logic completely, and even agreeing with some of it—but not to the point where I could commit myself to obvious falsehood. And, rather than frightening tourists away, it seemed to me that talk of murder would only increase the Garden's notoriety and attract even more visitors.

"You know this wasn't suicide," I said.

"I know that," the abbot replied. "You know that. Lt Poom knows that. We'll get to the bottom of it, I can assure you. But we're not going to go around telling folks he was murdered because you'll scare people off. We've worked hard in this community—all the menfolk have helped build this Garden, helped promote it, maintain it. It's the only thing we've got in these parts to keep people coming to our neck of the woods."

He seemed to be waiting for me to reassure him that I wouldn't be running around and spouting the "m" word—murder.

"It's your own affair," I said. "Of course, you must do what you think is right."

His smile told me he was going to do just that one way or the other.

"This is two 'suicides' now," I said, somewhat more angrily than I intended. "What is going on here?"

"That's what you're supposed to find out. That's why you were sent, isn't it?"

"But you must have some idea."

"Father Ananda, I'm a busy man. I've got eighty monks, a dozen nuns to look after. A school. The Garden—I've got about fifty crocodiles that have to be fed everyday. Do you know what that's like, coming up with that much food? I've got budget meetings, staff meetings, ordinations, dharma classes. I've got a refugee repatriation program to oversee. I've got a lot to do, in other words. What do you expect from me?"

"I expect you to care if you've got a murderer walking around here."

"A murderer?"

"Someone killed this man."

"And we'll get to the bottom of it."

"And someone killed Sister Moi."

"You have no proof of that."

"Not yet.

"If she was murdered, then I'm sure you'll figure that out too. Now excuse me."

FOUR

Back at the scene, Lt Poom was standing over the body, watching as two monks prepared to move it to the monastery's death room, where it would be bathed and prepared for the funeral rites. There was a hard look in Poom's eyes, but also something else—a bit of fear? I could not tell. They were the eyes of a man who was in over his head.

Before they took Brother Pandito away, I checked the pockets of his robes, finding what I expected to find—another note. *Garden 10 pm.* Written in the same hand as the one given to Sister Moi. I also found a small knife, which struck me as odd—unless Pandito had brought it because he expected some sort of trouble, had wanted some way to defend himself. I thought about the skin scrapings under Pandito's fingernails and frowned.

Lt Poom seemed to want to speak to me, yet not in front of the monks, so we waited until they carried Pandito's body away.

"You were sent by the Maha Thera Samakhom, weren't you?" Poom asked.

I nodded.

"If I told you something in confidence, can you keep your mouth shut about it?"

"Of course."

"When Sister Moi died, I had my doubts . . . about whether it was suicide . . . or not. I went along with the abbot. You know about the abbot, don't you?"

From the way he asked the question, I knew immediately what he was getting at—that the abbot's brother was a mafia higher-up, an "influential person," as we called them. One of the "unusually rich."

"I do," I said.

"Well, now I'm being railroaded again, and I can't say I like it much. But there isn't much I can do about it. If you stick your neck out, I suppose it's only fair to warn you that there might be consequences—these people don't fool around."

"No, they don't," I agreed. "But they're not above the law."

He laughed, somewhat bitterly.

"What's going on here?" I asked, hoping he would trust me, that he would open up, would give me a chance.

"I can't say," he said, shaking his head. It was clear that there was much he could say, but didn't dare. "Sister Moi tried to tell me once, but I wouldn't listen—I didn't want to know. I told her not to get involved, to go to Bangkok if she wanted to be a nun, not to stay here. She wouldn't listen. I wish she hadn't been so stubborn."

"And what about Pandito, her brother?"

"He came to see me yesterday, wanted to talk to me. I refused."

"Why?"

He grabbed another stalk of the long grass, started chewing on it, letting his eyes rest on some point in the distance—one of the Garden's many trees or exhibits, I could not tell. "I have two boys and a girl, Father Ananda."

I waited for him to continue.

"Surely I don't have to explain," he added, giving me a meaningful look. "Not to you anyway."

An icy hand took hold of my gut.

Of course.

In the days before I had become a Buddhist monk, I had been a police officer, like him. I'd had a wife and son. I had just been transferred to the anti-narcotics squad. We'd made a huge raid, got our picture in the paper. The next day the "influential people" that we had embarrassed—and whose drugs we had taken—sent two men round on a motorbike who had shot my wife and son to death in the driveway to our small house.

We hit them. They hit us.

No, he did not have to explain the forces at work when it came to mafia types. Poom was saying that he did not want his family to come to harm over something he had no control over anyway, that he was not willing to stick his neck out.

"I understand," I said, my voice somewhat weak. I was surprised at how the memory of the deaths of my wife and son still affected me, still brought out an ache in my heart that had never quite stopped.

"So you see the spot I'm in," he went on. "You say this is a murder. I say it's a suicide. That's what I have to say. That's what's going in my report. I'm a proud man, Father Ananda. I want to do my job well. But I can't. I don't want any harm to come to my family."

"I understand," I said again.

"That file you were asking about? For Sister Moi? It's missing now. Someone took it from my office, I guess. I was going to show it to you anyway, as long as you'd keep your mouth shut about it, but now it's gone."

"Don't worry about it," I said, feeling a bit disingenuous.

"Watch your back, Father Ananda"

He walked away.

FIVE

Jak had been sitting on the edge of the path, in a shady spot, watching these goings-on with less than enthusiasm. It was providing food for meditation on mortality, I suspected.

"What happened, Pho?" he asked as I approached.

"I don't know," I said.

"Did he kill himself?"

"I don't think so."

"I saw something," he said, getting to his feet. "Maybe it's nothing. But maybe you should have a look, just in case it might be important. It's just over here."

He led me along the footpath that led into the Garden of Falsehoods exhibit, and stopped at a row of small bushes. Hanging from one of the tangled boughs was a set of brown prayer beads.

"They must belong to someone," Jak said, looking up to me.

"You're quite right," I said. I pulled them away from the branch.

"Pho, you shouldn't touch them!" Jak exclaimed—monks were never supposed to touch any object that had not been expressly offered to them.

"Some rules are meant to be broken," I said, holding the beads carefully and looking at them, wondering if perhaps they might belong to a murderer. Given the number of people traipsing through the exhibits each day, it was hard to imagine such a set of beads had not already been found—unless they had been lost the night previous by someone fleeing the scene, or at least someone who had been there, and who might know what actually had happened.

Jak, as if reading my thoughts, smiled. "You think the killer dropped them?"

"Perhaps," I said.

SIX

Brother Pandito's body was moved to the death room, the place where corpses were prepared for funeral rites.

In life, he'd been handsome, strong, in an upcountry sort of way, someone who, as a youth, had probably spent day after day in a rice field, working from sun-up to sun-down, planting shoots, harvesting, tilling, digging water trenches to keep the rice paddies properly irrigated.

I watched as the monks bathed Pandito's body, prepared the coffin, got the body inside the coffin, having first sprinkled the obligatory tea leaves in the bottom of the coffin that absorbed moisture and reduced some of the smell. After the body laid in state for awhile in the funeral *sala,* the coffin would be nailed up. That evening the funeral rites would begin.

Almost as soon as word of his death had gotten around, cars starting showing up in the Garden of Hell parking lot—local folks, the family of Brother Pandito, the curious.

The preparations and rituals were tended to carefully because Brother Pandito had died violently—whether by his own hand, or that of someone else, it made no difference. Those who die violently have a tendency to remain close to their bodies, confused at the sudden separation between themselves and the body they once inhabited. It's up to family and friends to now convince the spirit to move on, to take another birth somewhere else. What the family doesn't want is for the spirit to hang around, angry, frustrated, lonely, hurting. And so food and drink will be offered to Pandito every morning and every evening. His family and friends will gather to mourn and commiserate. And after three days of this, his coffin and body will placed in a crematorium, reducing the life he once lived to a pile of ashes that will be kept in an urn. With no body to fixate on, and with the love and encouragement of his family, relatives, and friends, Pandito will hopefully move on to whatever rebirth awaits him.

That's the hope, at any rate. Our folklore is filled with stories of those who didn't move on—who remain behind to haunt and terrify, to seek revenge against their killers.

If Pandito was going to choose that route, I hoped he would give me a clue or two as to who his killer was.

SEVEN

I conducted interviews after lunch. The abbot and Brother Kusalo assisted me. I asked that each and every monk, starting from the novices and moving upward through the ranks, come before me for an interview. I also requested that they bring their extra set of robes so that I could examine all the robes and determine whether any of them had a piece torn out that would match up with the piece of monk's robe that I had found in Sister Moi's file.

So the monks came forward, one by one. None, it seemed, had seen or heard anything unusual the previous night when the murder had taken place. I didn't use the "murder" word while interviewing them; I merely inquired as to their whereabouts, and whether they had taken note of anything suspicious or unusual the previous day and night. I then asked to look at their spare set of robes, and then at the robes they were wearing.

All monks are expressly allowed to possess needle and thread, for the purpose of keeping one's robes in shape. At times, the hem will come loose, or the robes will tear on a tree branch or some other such thing. So now, as the monks filed past, I saw lots of patched robes, and one or two that I thought could be possible matches.

The majority of the monks had easily verifiable alibis, usually their *kuti* partner, who could vouch for their whereabouts. These included Panya and Subha, who conveniently alibied each other.

Panya was a big man with a round face and small, piggish eyes. He did not take kindly to my inquiring about Sister Moi and their relationship.

"There was no *relationship*," he snorted angrily. "Don't believe everything you hear, especially around this place."

"Why did Moi accuse you of raping her?" I asked.

"How should I know? The woman was a baboon."

"So you didn't have a relationship with her at all?"

"No."

He regarded me with serious, unflinching eyes, as if defying me to dare contradict him.

I did not. I let the matter go; there were more important things to investigate at that moment.

The few monks without alibis were senior monks, each older than the last, each looking as though they might have trouble walking as far as the Garden of Hell, much less stringing up a young monk in one of the exhibits.

It was that, of course—the physical mechanics of the act—that pointed to a man being the killer. I did not see how it could be otherwise. It had to have been a man, someone strong, someone capable of committing such a crime. None of the nuns would have been able to "hang" Brother Pandito, unless I was very much mistaken.

I had a curious interview with a monk named Nandapanya. Kusalo whispered into my ear that Nandapanya had argued with Pandito yesterday though he couldn't say precisely what the argument had been about.

Brother Nandapanya was a plain-spoken man, large, his chest thick, his hands used to hard work. He was, he said, one of the gardeners who helped keep the Garden of Hell clean and maintained.

"I'm wondering where you were last night," I said.

"I was in the Garden," he said, staring at me with curious eyes.

"You were in the Garden? Do you know what time?"

"It was late, I know that. I was meditating near the crocodile enclosure."

"Did you see anyone in the Garden? Hear anything unusual?" I asked.

He nodded quite readily. "Heard some shouting."

"Shouting?"

Again he nodded.

"Did you go to investigate?"

"Not really. It wasn't all that unusual—kids are always scaling the wall, getting inside at night, meeting their friends or their girl-friends, or whatever. I just thought a couple of them were having a fight about something. Couldn't hardly hear it anyway."

"Did you catch any of the words?"

"No, sorry, I didn't."

He seemed very honest, very straightforward. He maintained eye contact, did not appear to have anything to hide.

I sprang my next question on him, wanting to see if he would be surprised. "You argued with Brother Pandito yesterday, didn't you?"

He nodded, shrugged, did not seem as if he cared one way or the other about the matter. "Pandito was complaining about the trees in the Garden. He wanted some of them removed. I told him it was quite a job to remove trees, but, as usual, he didn't care. Said I was lazy."

"Why did he want to cut down trees?"

"He wanted to make another exhibit. He's been going on about that for a long time. We've had that argument about a dozen times already. Wasn't really nothing new. And it wasn't worth killing him over."

I watched him for long moments. He seemed utterly sincere, as if he knew he had done nothing wrong and had nothing to worry about. Which meant that he was probably innocent—or a very good liar.

That was the problem with interviews. We could be very good liars if we wanted to. It had to do with face: to admit to something shameful would lead to losing face, and there are some of us who will do anything—anything at all—to avoid a loss of face, even if that includes outright lies.

"These voices," I said, returning to the previous subject. "Did you go investigate afterwards?"

"Not really. During my meditation, I walked the circuit around the park, but I wasn't really paying much attention."

"Did you see anything?"

"A flash of orange, yes, I did. Thought it was strange for one of the monks to be in the park that late at night. But then some of them do meditations among the exhibits like I do, so it wasn't that unusual."

"A flash?"

"Like he was running away, or didn't want me to see him. Maybe he didn't have permission to be out so late. Probably didn't—was probably one of the novices fooling around like they do. And you know how that is."

I did.

"Anything else unusual happen last night?" I asked.

He shrugged.

"Can anyone verify your whereabouts?"

"I was by myself."

As he walked away, I put him down on my list of suspects. Not a strong possibility, though, rather a place to start should nothing else turn up.

After several more interviews, a monk named Silapalo came before us. Kusalo whispered in my ear that Silapalo and Pandito had fought often—their animosity was well known in the monastery.

Silapalo looked at me with uncertain eyes.

"I'm wondering where you were last night," I said.

Lips can lie, but faces generally cannot. We betray ourselves in countless ways. Sometimes it's more profitable to simply watch a person than to make any effort to listen to what they are saying. I was reminded of this as I watched Silapalo speak.

"I went to my *kuti*," he said, rolling his eyes up and to the right, which meant he was trying to recall something—or make something up on the spot.

"What time was that?" I asked.

He raised his right hand and wiped at his chin, his fingers covering his lips. That's generally a signal that what is coming next is most likely a lie. It's as if the fingers are trying to stop the mouth from doing something wrong.

"Just after the evening chants," he said.

"And what did you do?"

He shrugged. "I went to bed."

The way a person stands offers clues as to what they're really saying. To stand on two feet, back straight, hands at the side, indicates confidence, non-aggression. To bend one leg and put one's weight on the other indicates uncertainty, doubt, as if the body was unconsciously preparing to flee, should that become necessary. That's an odd response for one with nothing to hide, and that's what Silapalo was doing now. His behavior was almost the opposite of Nandapanya's.

Gestures also have their own language. Clenching the hands into fists indicates anger, aggression. Wringing the hands together, fidgeting, checking pockets, all convey doubt, uncertainty. Putting a hand on the back of the neck also indicates doubt, questioning, and yet sincerity. Wiping at the eyebrow indicates stress, a bit of fear and nervousness.

"Did you do anything else last night?" I asked.

He wiped at his eyebrow, not letting me see his eyes—when someone won't give you their eyes, it generally means they're afraid of being exposed or found out, or that they're lying.

"I went to sleep," he said, keeping his eyes lowered. Then he raised them to look at me, as if to see whether I believed this or not.

"From what I understand, you didn't like Brother Pandito, did you?"

His right hand balled itself into a fist. He quickly put his hands in the robes of his pockets, again not looking at me.

"Of course I didn't," he said. "Everybody knows that. But that doesn't mean I killed him."

"Is that what you think this is about?" I asked.

He looked up to me now, giving me his eyes, frowning, as if he didn't understand.

Murder was precisely what we were talking about, but it's often helpful to confuse and misdirect, which provokes just the sort of response Silapalo was giving me now, providing a contrast to his other responses. This response was honest, genuine: he was puzzled. His other responses indicated deception.

"Can anyone vouch for your whereabouts?" I asked. "Your *kuti* partner, for example?"

"I don't have one," he said, continuing to look at me, showing plainly by his expression that he was telling the truth. Then he lowered his eyes before adding, "I went to bed. I was tired."

The beads that Jak had found that morning were still in my pocket. I now took them out and showed them to Silapalo.

"Are these yours?"

"Yes," he said. "I misplaced them."

I handed him the beads. "I found those beads this morning near the crime scene—you must have dropped them there last night."

He shot me a nervous glance and his lower lip trembled.

"I didn't kill him," he said, now looking at me. I could see he was afraid, troubled, that he knew something about what had gone on, but wasn't about to tell me. I suspected that he was telling me the truth—that he hadn't killed Brother Pandito. But he knew who did, or at least had his suspicions, or he might have even participated.

"I may want to talk to you again sometime," I said.

He turned away quickly and was gone from sight.

I put his name down on my list.

EIGHT

At the office, I asked Brother Kusalo to show me the file on Brother Pandito. He did. Abbot Uddi was in his office, door closed, and Kusalo went about his chores quietly, as if walking on eggshells, as if he knew the boss was in a bad mood. And no doubt he was. Murder will do that to you.

There was nothing much to see in Pandito's file: an application, a two-by-two-inch photo, a medical certificate testifying to his sound health.

Next I rechecked the files for Brother Silapalo and Brother Nandapanyo. Both were locals, had grown up in the nearby village. Neither had handwriting that matched the notes. There were no reports of misconduct or health concerns.

I looked at Kusalo, sitting in his office chair, and frowned.

He frowned in return.

His desk was a bit of a mess. Papers were piled haphazardly here and there. The phone was up to its buttons in this, that, and the other thing. There was even a bottle of chili powder in the mess, along with knick-knacks, rubber bands, an overly large stapler, an old bottle holding pens and pencils—Kusalo was not the most organized person in the world, that was for sure.

"What's going on in this place?" I asked him very quietly.

He offered a confused look as if he couldn't say what he wanted to say. He glanced at the door to the abbot's office, raised his eyebrows, made a funny sort of face. With the abbot around, in other words, he wasn't at liberty to say much.

"I could really use your help," I said. "People are dying here. Doesn't that concern you?"

He sat forward, leaned closer to me. "The only people dying are the ones who cause trouble." He added a meaningful look to this statement, suggesting that it was a warning.

"And they're going to keep dying until a stop is put to it."

"And you're the one who's going to do that?" he asked.

"It's better than doing nothing," I replied.

"You don't have to live here, do you?" he asked. He had a point.

"But if you know something, why not just tell me?" I pressed.

"I don't know anything, Father Ananda. I'm just as clueless as you are. I just don't want to get myself in trouble."

Fair enough. A coward's way out, of course, but even so.

"I'd like you to give me a tour of the nun's facilities," I said, "and I'd like to also see where the children in the repatriation program are kept. Are you busy?"

He was not. He led Jak and myself through the complex, which was surrounded on all sides by concrete walls. In the back of the complex there was a small gate. We went through this gate, emerged into the nun's quarters, which consisted of a row of *kuti*, a building that served as a shower and a bathroom, another small open-air *sala* that served as the nuns' meeting place and meditation area, plus a place to cook. All this was surrounded by concrete walls.

There were about a dozen nuns altogether, Kusalo said.

"This area is off-limits, of course," Kusalo said. "Monks are not supposed to come back here for any reason. The nuns, on the other hand, are free to come and go—they do the cooking in our kitchen, the clean-up, chores, that sort of thing."

As befits their low status, I thought, but did not say.

Blue pipe extended beneath the gate, bringing in a lone source of tap water. As well, an electrical cord that snaked over the top of the concrete wall dividing the monastery from the nun's quarters provided a source of electricity. Apart from those two concessions, the nuns lived a very primitive life indeed, cooking their own meals on gas stoves, washing dishes in plastic buckets, collecting rainwater in earthen jugs, washing their clothes by hand.

Sister Mettha came from the *sala*, offered a *wai* of respect.

"Sister," I said, nodding a greeting.

"What can we do for you, Father Ananda?"

"I just wanted to see your living arrangements. Do you find everything satisfactory?"

"We do, yes," she said. "We cook and clean for the monks, and in exchange, they provide water and electricity. It is enough for us."

Out behind their row of *kuti* were open fields, some given over to rice harvesting, some heavy with palm and coconut trees. Wind swept in from the fields. Much farther down along the concrete wall that closed off the monastery proper from the rest of the world was another set of buildings which I guessed to be dorms for the foreign children that were processed here.

"I'd like to see what you do, exactly, with the children," I said.

"For the repatriation project," Kusalo added helpfully.

"Tell me about that," I said to Sister Mettha as we walked down the path next to the wall that looked to be well-trampled by numerous feet over a long period of time.

It was Kusalo, though, who did the talking. Apparently he thought Sister Mettha incapable of it. "The children are either repatriated or sent to one of the border refugee camps," he said. "It depends. Cambodians will be sent home. Burmese will go to the camps. We try to identify them, reunite them with their families, if possible."

The concrete buildings were functional, not built for style or aesthetics. They looked more like army barracks than dorms for children.

"Who deals with the paperwork?" I asked.

"I handle all of it myself," Kusalo said.

"Why are there so many children?"

"Do you know much about refugees, Father Ananda?"

I did not.

"We handle all the ones being sent up from Bangkok. That's why we have so many. A lot of these kids aren't orphans, really. Their parents have abandoned them. Some of the older ones go to Bangkok looking for work, get sent to us instead. A lot of them are picked up off the streets. I think the important thing is getting them away from Bangkok, because there's already too many of them there, to start with, and they just don't have the facilities to handle everyone. Anyway, they're not citizens, don't have paperwork, don't belong in this country to start with. Something's got to be done about them."

The majority of the nuns were here, among the buildings, which were themselves surrounded by a tall fence with barbed wire at the top, making it look like a fortress or a prison. The children were kept in the dorms. Most were lying on beds, or sitting together on the floor playing. They looked up when we entered, immediately became quiet. They seemed frightened, unsure of themselves and of this world they now inhabited, of what was to become of them.

It was not lost on me that most of the children staring back at us were young girls, ranging from perhaps eight to twelve years of age. There were a few boys, too, but not nearly as many.

One girl, sitting on a bed nearby, clutched a tattered-looking teddy bear to her thin chest. She looked to be about ten. Her eyes were dark pools of misery, sadness, fright. She clung to the teddy bear as if it were a talisman against evil. A dirty dress hung from her shoulders. There was a bruise on her right arm.

As if explaining, Kusalo said, "They can be quite shaken up when they get here. We give them a few days to rest, recover, get used to the idea of being sent home, or sent to a camp. Communicating with them is difficult. One of the nuns speaks Khmer, but that's about it. She can identify the Cambodians. The others we have to sometimes take a guess, do our best. If we can't make a determination, we'll send them on to the Immigration Department, but they already have so many detainees at Immigration, and their facilities are not designed for children anyway, so we try to avoid that, if at all possible."

I continued to look at the girl on the bed, clutching her teddy. She continued to look at me. There was a pleading look in her eyes, something that transcended language barriers, a very simple human thing, an emotion easily communicated from one human being to another with nothing more than a gaze.

"And what about her?" I asked, nodding in the girl's direction.

"She's Cambodian," Sister Mettha offered. "She'll be sent back soon. She's a long way from home."

"She seems frightened."

"Many of them are," Mettha agreed. "Afraid of us, of what's going to happen to them. We do our best to comfort them, to make this as easy as possible. But of course it isn't easy."

The girl got up, approached me but did not touch me. She only stood before me, looking up at me with her large, sad eyes.

Sister Mettha immediately began fussing, trying to get her to go sit down, but the little girl would not.

I felt somewhat awkward yet sorry for the girl.

"Who's the nun who speaks Khmer?" I asked.

One of the nuns—a small woman, youngish, flat-faced—presented herself.

"What is this girl's name?"

"La-or," she replied. "She's having a hard time with this . . . as you can see."

"Tell her it's going to be alright."

The woman obliged.

"Ask her where she's from, how she got here."

The nun spoke in Khmer, waited for a response, which was a loud outpouring, punctuated with tears. The girl said she was in the jungle with her family, was taken away by men, was put on a truck, had wound up here. She said the men were bad, had done bad things to her.

"What kind of bad things?" I asked.

The nun doing the translation now hesitated.

"Ask her," I said forcefully. "What kind of bad things?"

"These kids tell you so many stories," the nun replied quietly. "It's hard to believe them sometimes. I think they just want you to feel sorry for them—they'll say anything if they think you'll let them stay in this country."

"Ask her," I repeated.

She did.

La-or said the man were mean, had slapped her, had hit her several times because she wouldn't stop crying.

The nun conveyed this quietly, with a resigned air.

"She's been abused," I said.

Sister Mettha stepped forward. "Most of them have, in one way or another, Father Ananda—that's why we're trying to send them home, or get them to a camp. You'll hear a lot of horror stories if you stick around long enough, I can promise you that."

La-or continued to stare at me, as if pleading. I felt sorry for her, but also felt as though there were things not being said here—mysteries, secrets. The place seemed shrouded with darkness and shadow.

I wanted to comfort La-or, but could not. I wondered what it would be like to have a daughter like La-or, a small, innocent, trusting soul who looked up to you for warmth and protection. How could any decent man abuse such a child? How was it that we humans could do such things to helpless children?

NINE

Jak was quiet, reserved, had that peculiar sort of frown he wears when he's feeling bad about something. We were walking back to our *kuti* to take a rest after the morning's goings-on.

"What is it?" I asked quietly

"Pho?" he replied, looking up at me.

"You're thinking about something," I said. "You've got that look on your face."

He turned his face away from me, but not before I saw a slight grimace pass across his features.

I had fought very hard to have Jak accepted as a novice at our monastery. Most abbots don't like physical deformities, and some won't accept would-be monks who have them, regardless of whether the deformity has anything to do with whether one can live the homeless life or not. And the Lord Buddha most definitely never said that a boy who had suffered from polio as a child and had a deformed leg because of it would not be able to follow his teachings, or comprehend his Four Noble Truths, or embark on the path that led to nirvana.

Trouble was, any sort of abnormality or deformity, even being an orphan, for that matter, was considered the result of bad karma from a previous life. One was being punished for something one did in a previous life. One endured harsh conditions because one deserved it, one had earned it by actions in a previous life, and the karma was working itself out in this one.

Not only was such an idea very un-Buddhist, it reflected an extremely inaccurate understanding of what the Lord Buddha taught on the subject of karma. Karma, as the Lord Buddha taught, was an ongoing thing: if we do bad things, then bad things will result. Yet, if we do good things, good things will result. Karma is "fixable" in that way. True enough, one may be suffering in this life from bad karma, yet one can also take to the path of doing good, and thus change that karma, or at least exhaust it.

Even so, it remained popular and convenient to put the blame for someone's misfortune squarely on their own shoulders. If you were poor, it was because you were stingy in your previous life. If you were an orphan, it was because you didn't appreciate your parents in a previous life. If you were murdered, it was because you were a murderer in your previous life. It was a sort of shorthand that absolved bystanders of any guilt or responsibility for those less fortunate. Why, after all, should one care about the poor, when it's obviously their own fault that they're poor? If a woman was raped, well, it was her fault—she was just reaping her bad karma. She might have been a rapist in her previous life. Who could tell?

This sort of thinking also provided convenient absolution for the rich and well-off to glory in their wealth and privilege, since these things were also the result of karma—good karma. They had obviously been exceptional people in their previous lives, and now they were being rewarded. Why should they feel guilty for their good fortune?

This sort of perversion of the Lord Buddha's teachings was so deeply entrenched in some quarters that it was hard to combat.

Thus, when I had sought permission for Jak to take the robes, I had stumbled upon the suggestion that he was not fit for the robes because he was "a cripple"—and everyone knows that cripples are suffering from the fruit of their bad actions in a previous life.

I'd had a somewhat heated argument with the abbot when he spouted this nonsense at me. He assured me that he didn't believe any such thing himself, was only trying to make me understand what others believed, and why they would object to Jak taking the robes. It was akin to the same sort of thinking that had declared women were not capable of achieving enlightenment simply because they were women, and thus there was no point in their taking to the robes—they were only fooling themselves and wasting their time. Women, of course, were too interested in families, children, relationships, to ever get serious about the dharma.

At any rate, now that Jak *had* taken the robes, I feared he wasn't doing very well with the homeless life and I felt like I was standing by, watching him fail, watching the things that would eventually lead to his dismissal and I couldn't help him, I couldn't get through to him.

I had never been an orphan, so it was not possible for me to understand how it felt, how hard it must be to be parentless, to be without a man and a woman who loved you more than life itself. I wanted very much to understand, but I could not. I would never be able to.

I was also "normal"—I had no deformities. I got along easily with friends. My childhood wasn't filled with rejection and jeers. I wasn't mocked because I had a crippled limb. I wasn't laughed at, excluded, looked down upon. Thus I was never going to be able to understand what it had been like—what it was still like—to walk in Jak's shoes. I had no way of knowing how these hurts and wounds would work themselves out, whether Jak would be up to the task of confronting them and putting them to rest, or whether he would let them consume him with bitterness and anger.

"What is it?" I asked, genuinely concerned. "You know you can talk to me about anything. You know that, don't you?"

He ignored me, walked on ahead, not wanting to let me see his eyes.

I followed along dutifully—bewilderedly, in fact—until he at last took up roost beneath the bo tree where a series of concrete benches had been arranged. He sat down on one of these and put his bald head in his hands.

I sat down beside him.

"I miss my mum," he said miserably, before bursting into sudden tears.

I put an arm around his shoulder and sat with him. I didn't know what to say. His mother was dead. His father was dead. The death of his parents was like a hole in his heart, and nothing that I could ever say or do would fill it, nothing would make it better.

He cried for a long time.

Had the scene with La-or upset him?

My own son's tears had produced a feeling similar to what was now gripping me: hopelessness, a sort of anger, a need to protect, a bit of bewildered silence. I would gladly take any sort of pain rather than have to watch a child suffer it.

Jak sobbed for the longest time. I did my best to comfort him, assuring him it would get better, in time, that the pain would lessen. It would, I knew—but the hole would never be filled. Any number of years could pass, but that hole would remain. That was part of the price of being human. When something you loved was taken away, there would always be a scar left behind to remind you of what had been lost, of what could be no more.

"I'm sorry, Pho," he said, when the worst of the tears had passed. "I know I'm not supposed to be attached, but I can't help it."

He sniffled miserably. I gave him my handkerchief.

"Who told you that you couldn't be attached to your own mother?" I asked.

"You know," he said, as if that explained everything, as if resorting to those words could solve the problems of the entire universe.

"No, I don't know," I replied. "You should honor your mother and her memory. Your mother brought you into this world, and made your life possible—made enlightenment possible, like the Tibetans say. There is no way to repay that debt except by loving her and honoring her memory. And that's what your tears do—you honor her. She must have been a good woman, a good mother."

He wiped at his eyes, nodding—then started to cry again.

"I just want to see her one more time," he said at length, trying to get hold of himself. "Is that too much to ask? Just to see her one more time?"

It wasn't accepting reality as it was, but I didn't have the heart to point that out.

"Maybe we should indeed go see her," I said, taking his hand. "Maybe you should go pay respects to her memory."

"Could we?" he asked, his eyes going wide. "I mean, it's a long ways."

I nodded. It would take another day or two, by bus, to go back to his village, to the temple where his mother had been cremated and her ashes interred. But a couple of days wasn't much in the grand scheme of things and it might help him come to terms with what he had lost. And I was in no hurry to get back to Bangkok, in any event, not with all those love letters I was receiving and an increasingly agitated abbot waiting for me.

He wiped at his face, embarrassed by his tears, looked around to see if anyone had been watching. "I hate being a monk," he added.

Was that the real problem? Or was he trying to change the subject?

"I know," I said. And I did. It wasn't easy for young kids to adjust to life in the robes. "It isn't easy, is it?"

"It's just that dead monk . . . got me thinking about things."

As it would.

"And now you're investigating his death and you know what happened the last time."

"Nothing's going to happen to us," I said, trying to sound more certain than I felt.

"I mean, if they kill you, I don't know what I'm going to do," he blurted out. Then he promptly began to cry again.

After several minutes, he said, "I'm sorry."

"It's all right," I said.

For long moments, he stared at the ground in front of him, his lips moving as if he wanted to speak, to say something. But he remained silent.

I tried to think of something to say, but each phrase sounded more ridiculous than the previous one, so I said nothing.

"I was thinking about that nun," he said, speaking so softly I could hardly hear him. "Pho, if I did that, would I go to hell?"

The breathe got caught in my throat. Was he pondering suicide? He didn't take his eyes away from me and I could see that he was very serious indeed.

"Are you asking me what I would think if you committed suicide?" I asked quietly.

He took his eyes away and put a hand to his mouth.

"What if I can't stand it?" he asked, glancing at me. "What if it's too much? What if I just decide . . ."

His voice trailed off and he didn't finish his sentence.

I felt sick.

"I mean, you don't know what it's like," he said, animated. "All these people staring at me. Everywhere I go, people are staring and staring and watching me. And sometimes they just stare at me like I'm some animal in a zoo, like I'm too stupid to know they're staring at me, like I'm some monkey in a cage and they're just gawking at me because it's fun for them and they don't understand what it's like for me. I mean, what if I can't stand it any more?"

Teenagers are painfully self-aware, believing the whole world notices every little thing about them. Yet I could understand his point perfectly. Whenever we were together, I couldn't help but notice all the pairs of eyes trailing after him, watching him walk, watching the hitch in his step. Some of those eyes were filled with pity. Some were curious. Some were cruel. It annoyed me sometimes and I wasn't even the one they were looking at. It annoyed me that people could be so thoughtlessly rude.

"I hate this stupid leg!" he exclaimed suddenly, smacking a hand on his crippled leg, as if it was a bug he hoped to smash beneath his fist. "I hate my stupid life. I must have been a really bad person to take such a bad rebirth."

"And killing yourself is going to accomplish exactly what?" I asked.

"Well, at least they won't look at me any more," he said.

"That's true," I said. "Is that what you want, for people to stop looking at you?"

He nodded.

"Well, you're not going to get it," I said.

He made a face and looked away.

"Jak, the only thing I can tell you is that you need to take refuge in the Lord Buddha's teachings. You're in trouble now because you're not doing that."

"So it's my fault?" he demanded angrily.

"It's not about fault," I replied carefully. "What was the First Noble Truth that the Buddha taught?"

He shook his head and rolled his eyes, as if the Buddha's teachings were quite irrelevant.

"What was it?" I pressed.

"The truth about suffering," he said, grudgingly.

"The truth about suffering. Birth is suffering. Ageing, sickness, disease, death, to not get what one wants, to be united with that which is unpleasant—all these things are suffering. Isn't that what you are, Jak, 'united with that which is unpleasant'?"

He looked at me and frowned. He looked down at his leg and nodded.

"And what is the Second Noble Truth?" I asked.

"It's the truth about the origin of suffering," he answered, by rote, as if he had memorized it.

"And what is the origin?"

"*Tanha*," he said, using the Pali word for clinging and craving—literally, thirst.

"So what are you thirsting after?"

He shook his head and sighed. He didn't answer.

I answered for him. "You're thirsting for a world where people don't stare at you. You're thirsting for a healthy pair of legs, to be just like everybody else so that no one will look at you because you're different."

"Is that so wrong?" he asked, making a face.

I shook my head. "It isn't wrong, Jak. But it creates suffering. What are you doing right now? You're suffering. You're unhappy. You're talking about hanging yourself and wondering if you'll go to hell because of it."

"Pho, dammit," he said, his face taking on an expression of pain and unhappiness.

"I'm just giving you something to think about," I said, knowing he didn't want to hear any of this. "So what are the Third and Fourth Truths about? They're about the way to end suffering, the path that leads to the ending of suffering, aren't they? The Buddha is trying to say that if you cling to something—to some idea, to some wish, to some material possession, to physical beauty or bodily perfection—he's trying to say that you're going to create suffering for yourself. So don't cling to it. Accept it for what it is. Stop fighting it. Isn't that what you're doing? How are you going to get everyone in the world to stop staring at you? It will never happen. I want it to happen, for your sake, but it's not going to, and you know that. We both know that. You can't change all those people, but you can change yourself. You can decide that you don't care any more about people looking at you. You have the power to do that."

He began to cry again, a soft, miserable sort of moaning, wiping at his eyes.

I took his hand, afraid he would pull it away, but he did not. "Jak, these things I'm telling you, this is what the Buddha taught. And we keep talking about it now, twenty-five hundred years later, because it works, because it helps, because people feel better when they learn it, when they see how it works, when they see how to apply it to their own lives. If you want to feel better, this is the way to do it. That's what I'm trying to tell you. You're the one who made the decision that all these people staring at you is going to make you unhappy. You can make another decision. You can decide you don't care. You can decide these people are ignorant and not worth your time. You can decide that you're happy that everyone's looking at you, that you're the center of attention, that everywhere you go, everyone sees you—isn't that what some people want?"

"Oh, please," he said, wiping at his eyes.

"Isn't it?" I pressed. "These celebrities and famous people? Don't you think they suffer the same way you do? Don't you think they get sick of everyone looking at them? Or maybe they like it—who knows?"

He continued to frown.

"I feel sorry for you," I said. "I know people look at you. But what can you do about it? If you get angry at all of them, it's not going to change anything. People are still going to look at you. The only thing you can do is change yourself, change the way you think about it. The choice is up to you. You can let it get to you, or you can just shrug your shoulders and move on and not waste time about it."

He lowered his eyes and stared at the bench between us. "Pho, what if I can't be a monk?" he asked, not looking at me. "What if I fail? What if I do something and I'm instantly defeated? Are you still going to care about me?"

"Of course," I said.

He lowered his eyes.

TEN

Novice monks—those under the age of twenty, mostly—sat in their own circle, while the senior monks sat down together, cross-legged on the floor, to eat. The nuns had already laid out the food and water and fruit juices for lunch and were now nowhere to be seen. The abbot led us in a Pali chant and we ate in silence.

I was attached to food. I was doing my best not to be, but obviously I had a long way to go as far as food was concerned. I envied monks who could sit down to a meal and not be concerned about what they were eating, honestly and sincerely satisfied with whatever was offered. I longed for the day when I would be privy to such holy indifference.

Just last week Jak had told me of the story he'd heard about how the Lord Buddha had gone on an alms round, had accepted food from a man suffering from leprosy—and while offering the food, the leper's thumb happened to fall off into the Buddha's bowl and the Buddha was supposed to have eaten it, since it had been "offered."

Jak was full of such stories, each a bit less refined than the last, but that one was new to me and I had told him that I doubted very much whether it was actually true.

But the intent of the story, I suspect, was to instill in the listener the idea that one ought to be indifferent to the food one is offered—food is nourishment to the body and nothing more and one should be grateful for whatever nourishment is provided, not attached to tastes and sensations of the palate. Good or bad, pleasant or foul, one should simply eat and be done with it.

While I could agree with that sentiment, practicing it was another matter.

Thus it was with a fair bit of trepidation that I stared into my bowl, wondering what the nuns had concocted that could smell so strange and look even worse. But I ate it without complaint, although I was grateful for the small portion and did not ask for seconds.

Perhaps if I remained at Wat Yai for any length of time, I might make some progress in my detachment efforts.

ELEVEN

That afternoon, Jak and I joined the monks in the funeral *sala* for the funeral chants for Brother Pandito.

A multitude of cars sat in the parking lot and along the road out front. Pandito's mother and father were there, dressed in black and white, as were all the other mourners. There were young men and women congregating nearby and I suspected these were brothers and sisters of the deceased, or cousins, or close family.

A great many wreaths had been sent, each hanging from an easel and bearing the name of the family that had sent it, arranged on either side of the coffin, which was up front and raised on pedestals.

Judging from the crowd, Pandito and his family were well known in the community.

There would be three days of this. His family would bring food and water for Pandito in the mornings. In the late afternoons they would gather again at the *sala* to receive visitors. Food and drink (including the alcoholic kind, but kept under the tables) would be in abundance. Men would stand around outside the *sala* smoking cigarettes and talking about their jobs, their families, their lives. The women would congregate around the large couch situated in the middle of the funeral hall where the deceased's parents and immediate family sat. Rows of chairs behind this couch would seat mourners.

As each group of mourners arrived, they went up to the coffin where a huge candle burned. Next to this was a large urn for incense sticks. Mourners would take four—three in honor of the Lord Buddha, his teachings, and the community of monks that he had left behind, and one for the deceased—and light them to pay homage, putting them in the large urn with the many others. A more detached part of my brain reminded me that the incense sticks were helpful when it came to masking the smell of death.

For three days this would continue, then, after a final set of special chants and a sermon from the abbot, the coffin would be taken down from its pedestals and carried counterclockwise three times around the crematorium outside, before being taken up the crematorium steps in preparation for the cremation. The coffin would be opened for the family to have one last look at their loved one. Flowers made of sandalwood or paper would be placed inside the coffin, then on top of it by mourners, before the whole lot was put into the crematorium and set on fire.

There would be a great deal of crying, but also of coming together, of being supported by the community during this difficult time. There would be lots of food, drink, talk. The children would busy themselves with whatever games they could come up with and sometimes their boisterous laughing and screaming would have to be quieted. It was a sad occasion, but also very much a family occasion. Death, after all, was no stranger. Every family and community had to contend with it.

After the chants that evening I asked Kusalo to show me Pandito's *kuti*. Jak and I followed as Kusalo led us through the darkening evening to one of the *kuti* out in back.

I went inside the structure by myself. A *kuti* is a bungalow, basically, a one-room dwelling whose purpose—for a Buddhist monk—is either to sleep or to meditate. The *kuti* is supposed to reflect that, which Pandito's did. There was little more than a mat with a blanket, an old electric fan, a small bookcase with books, a plastic container filled with an extra set of robes, an umbrella standing in one corner.

The *kuti* itself was up on stilts, as most are, to keep its occupant away from flooding during the monsoon rains and to keep away from snakes and spiders and other wildlife that often hazard by. This doesn't always work out as planned, but it's safer than being on the ground.

Of course, I won't soon forget the rainy season of three year's back when I woke one morning to discover an enormous python curled up beneath my *kuti*. It had apparently gotten itself into the midst of the big city during a bout of flooding and had somehow or other decided to take up residence at Wat Mahanat. It was sick—that was obvious. Considering the sort of filthy floodwaters it must have swam through to get to Wat Mahanat, I was not surprised. It did little more than lie there for several days. Then one morning it was gone.

Inside Pandito's *kuti*, I thought about that python, wondered if Pandito might have his own tale to tell about *kuti* and wildlife. Goodness knows we all did.

I looked under his mat, hoping to find something—anything—but to no avail. Pandito was certainly not a packrat, had few possessions to speak of. I sat down on the wooden floor to rummage through the contents of the plastic container. I found underwear, robes, two T-shirts, a grand total of three baht in one-baht coins, an old pamphlet on the virtues of a vegetarian diet, little else.

Frustrated, I got to my feet and began to examine the walls, hoping to find something or other stuck in a corner or tacked to the wall. But that too proved fruitless.

How could I solve a murder if there were no clues to go on? It was maddening.

Based on what I knew of monks, it was safe to say that each had his secrets. And the only place to keep those secrets was in a *kuti* or a dormitory cell. I looked around once more at Pandito's dwelling. Where did he keep his secrets? Where did he keep that extra stash of money (for "emergencies")? Or that photo of his parents or an old girlfriend, or other bits of the world that were supposed to have been left behind when one took the robes?

I looked through all the books, one by one. Had he stuffed something inside one of them? Apparently not, as I discovered the hard way. I moved the bookcase, looked behind it. Nothing. In one corner of his *kuti* was a small stand with a Buddha image sitting on top of it. I examined the stand, lifted the Buddha, checked beneath his bronze self, came up empty-handed.

Come on, Pandito. Help me out here!

The only thing left was the mattress, which I had already checked. Now I hunched down on the floor, examining it again. There was nothing beneath it, nothing underneath the top sheet, but as I examined the mat more closely, I saw a slit—

Success!

Inside the small cavity created by the slit I found a small stash of business cards, six hundred-baht notes, a pack of chewing gum.

I put the business cards in my pocket, left the other items as they were and rejoined Kusalo and Jak outside.

TWELVE

"Pho, I'm scared. Please—*please!*—can't we sleep somewhere else?"

I looked at my young charge and frowned. Dark had fallen and we were preparing to retire.

"What's wrong with the *kuti* we're staying in?" I asked, perplexed.

"If someone wanted to kill us like they killed that monk, they would know exactly where to find us, wouldn't they?"

"Why would anyone want to kill us?"

He rolled his eyes, as if I were the densest person alive.

"Can't we stay in the dormitory?" he asked, pleading with his eyes. He was really rather scared that someone would come upon us in the night and do us in.

I had no such fear, but I could understand. Jak had already thwarted one attempt on my life in the past. He was probably not in any hurry for a sequel. He would be frightened that something like that might happen again, despite the odds against it.

"Okay," I said.

He rewarded me with a large smile full of teeth. "I'm not trying to be a bother, Pho," he said. "It's just that I'm scared."

"I know," I replied, motioning for him to lead the way.

"And Panya's ghost is probably hanging around too," he said.

That was always a possibility.

We soon found ourselves bedding down in the large open dormitory along with about a dozen junior monks. Mats were scattered here and there and there didn't seem to be any particular order or way of doing things.

Jak arranged our two mats right in the middle of the room as if he thought that might increase our chances of survival.

Perhaps it would, at that.

CHAPTER FOUR

*"You cannot fulfill your destiny by hanging on
to the qualities of youth."*
—The Sage's Tao Te Ching: A New Interpretation, #22

ONE

I rested for about an hour.

I hadn't told Novice Jak of my desire to see the Garden of Hell at night, especially around 10 p.m. or so, just to see what might be seen. And 10 p.m. seemed to be the magical hour when things happened at Wat Yai.

There were a few points I needed to satisfy myself on, such as whether the temple dogs would bark if a stranger wandered about at night, whether the bridge made of supposed human skulls would moan and groan if crossed at night, and whether or not much could be seen in the Garden at full dark. But I was also curious to see who might be prowling about and what they might be up to.

I rose quietly, making sure Jak was fast asleep—like most teens, he had no problem in that department. That was another one of youth's blessings that had left me long ago, which I hadn't missed until it was gone—the ability to actually fall asleep quickly, without a lot of tossing and turning.

I dug through my monk's bag for my torch, gripped it tightly.

As a monk, I could not wear a wristwatch. There were times, though, when one would come in handy. At any rate, each monastery has a gong tower and the ringing of the gong rouses, calls to chants, indicates meal times—there's no need for a watch. I had also discovered the curious fact that one's body generally knows what time it is anyway. I could usually guess the time, day or night, and be accurate to within a few minutes. As I tiptoed among the sleeping monks, I was guessing that it was about 10 p.m., or very close to it, but I wished I could be absolutely certain.

I made my way carefully to the door, eased it open, stepped outside. The night air was cool, blessedly so, and I paused for long moments to admire the brilliant night sky and its many stars. Living in the city, one didn't see many stars, least not the celestial kind, and there was something comforting about them. The moon was beginning to wane, but still providing plenty of light to see by and as my eyes adjusted, I took to the footpaths that wandered among the *kuti*.

All was quiet.

Here and there, dogs slumbered beneath *kuti* and paid no attention to me. A man in orange robes could be a common enough sight, yet temple dogs have a rather accurate sense of who belongs—and who doesn't. Still, they didn't bark. They didn't even so much as roll over or look at me.

I wandered up to the main buildings. The funeral *sala* was shut up now, Brother Pandito inside, today's rituals and mourning finished, tomorrow's awaiting. The temple was likewise locked, the parking lot for the Garden of Hell empty. I was feeling rather thirsty and went to the dining hall to see if there might be some water there, but it too was locked.

On the far side of the parking lot was the entrance to the Garden of Hell. I walked as quietly as I could across the gravel, hoping I would not be seen. Once at the entrance, I paused as I remembered the golden tree snakes—I dreaded the trip through their midst. Especially at night.

I don't like snakes. In fact, I'm terrified of them all out of proportion to any threat they might pose to me. It's completely irrational, I admit. I suppose it must have something to do with a childhood memory: I was once playing in a large water jar, which was empty, pretending that it was my house, when my older brother came along and threw in a perfectly harmless garden snake. I got out of that water jar so quickly one would have thought a space shuttle had taken off. The fact that the thing had landed in my lap and slithered across my bare leg had not helped matters in the slightest. And I had quite forgotten that the snakes one needs to be afraid of are the ones that won't get out of your way. If they go slithering off into the undergrowth, they're afraid of you; if they bask in the sun and don't give a damn about you, they're poisonous and likely to take a bite out of your hide for disturbing them. Cobras have even been known to go chasing after you if you upset them and they're much faster than they might look.

So now I paused. Did I really need to be prowling about this Garden at night? Could it wait? I used the torch to search the ground about me, expecting to see snakes. I saw nothing but the path between the trees. That didn't stop my mind from conjuring up all sorts of possible horrors.

Shuddering, knowing I would lose what little nerve I had if I allowed myself to think too much longer about the matter, I bowed my head low and hunched over, moving down the path between the trees as quickly as I could, dreading every second of it. My mind conjured up the feeling of a snake falling on my bare neck, slithering across it. I was afraid I would step on one or be bitten by one as I darted past. I had so spooked myself that by the time I got to the skull bridge, I ran across it, forgetting that it might trigger the recording and announce my presence to one and all.

I didn't care.

But the bridge made no sound and I was grateful.

I found myself in the Garden of Lust, and I slowed my footsteps, struggling to calm my nerves and get a hold of myself. I was acting like a child, not a man on the other side of fifty. I wiped at my forehead, trying not to think about the fact that I was going to have to run that gauntlet once more when I left.

The exhibit's large, somewhat barren tree stood in front of me, the one with thorns and the naked men trying to scale it to get to their naked mistresses at the top. In the moonlight, the tree looked forbidding, frightening even, as if there really were such trees in hell with such unfortunate men trying to scale them.

I walked slowly, alert now, peering about the mannequins, trees, and brush for any signs of life or movement. All was quiet.

I followed the path past the crocodile enclosure and down to the next exhibit, the Garden of Falsehoods. Under the moon's glow, the faces on the figurines took on grim, deadly appearances. Faces were thrown in sharp relief from light and shadow. The guardians seemed somehow larger, more menacing, their victims more pitiable and helpless. I saw grimaces, snarls, pain, despair.

Why had Pandito come here? And what had happened afterward? Who had he come to meet? Where, exactly, had he died ... and why had the killer tried to disguise his death as a suicide when it very obviously wasn't? Was I dealing with a stupid murderer who didn't have a clue about dead bodies and the secrets they can reveal to the observant eye?

I wandered to the next exhibit, the Garden of Cruelty, but not after spending an anxious minute peering about in the dark for the clearing where the tiger had been yesterday afternoon. The tiger was gone. As to where it had gone, I did not care, just as long as it was locked up somewhere and not roaming about free.

When I got to the Garden of Cruelty, I sighed with relief.

I did not believe much in hell. The Christians and Muslims had one. As if to outdo them, we Buddhists had came up with seven. Ours were not eternal and I simply could not wrap my mind around the idea that such places *could* be eternal—everlasting, created by a God as a means to punish eternally, with no chance of ever escaping it. What sort of God could create such a place? What crime could a man commit that would merit such overwhelming punishment? I had known a few souls who probably deserved a few hundred years of torment in a place like this Garden of Cruelty—being sawn in half by hell's guardians, having their eyes pecked out by vultures, or fingernails ripped off, or limbs chopped off, and all the other such things depicted around me—people such as Hitler, Stalin, Mao, Pol Pot. But there would have to come a point in time when their debt was paid, when they had sufficiently reaped the punishment of their own karma, their own behavior, when the cruelty they had inflicted on others had been sufficiently returned to them. There had to be hope of change, redemption, of second chances, no matter what a person had done. To assign a person to eternal torment seemed unimaginably cruel.

Hell might indeed be other people, but it was also a life not lived well, a life without happiness, without choices, a life that has become too burdensome to carry, to the point where some creatures long for non-existence and might even take their own life in the hopes of achieving it. The Lord Buddha said the two extremes must be avoided: clinging to existence as well as longing for non-existence. We had to find the path between them.

The Buddha had also taught that we created our own heavens and hells, in our own lives, crystallized into dogmas like the existence of a physical hell. All of these were mind-made, without real existence.

I sat down on the edge of a large chopping block where an unfortunate lady was being eviscerated by an animal-like creature. I breathed in deeply, trying to relax and calm my anxious thoughts, which were jumping about from subject to subject like a monkey on a tree in search of the perfect banana. There was no such banana, but that didn't stop the monkey from searching for it and disregarding all the perfectly acceptable alternatives he might come across in the process.

I was missing something vital—but what?

When I had been a police officer, years ago, my boss had been a gentleman named Pol Gen Pricha. Whenever I had a difficult case to unravel, I would go into his office and we would go over it, piece by piece. Time and again he had reminded me to "Follow the leads—all the rest is distraction."

Follow the leads.

But that was the problem—thus far, my leads had gone nowhere.

I frowned, looking at the poor lady on the table beside me, the strange animal ripping into her guts, her feeble hands trying to beat him off, copious amounts of blood everywhere.

I was missing something. Pandito had obviously been murdered, but the mechanics of it escaped me. Where had it been done? Here in the Garden? Somewhere else? If somewhere else, then the murderer had brought his body here—risky. He might very well have been seen. Far easier to entice Pandito into the Garden with a note. The note found in his pocket seemed to confirm that idea. That he had brought a knife with him suggested that he thought he might need protection, might be in danger. And obviously, he was right.

The marks on Pandito's neck suggested he had been strangled, perhaps with a piece of chain. Had he been strangled, then left to lie on the ground for a long enough period of time that blood would settle in his back and buttocks? Why such a long period of time? Why hadn't he been strung up straight away? Or did the killer have plenty of time to clean up after himself? Was he in no hurry to dispose of the body? Had he killed Pandito in a place where there was no fear of anyone stumbling across him?

If he had been murdered in this place, one could assume that some evidence of that crime would have been left behind. But if it had been, I couldn't find it.

I got to my feet and continued on, making the full circuit of the Garden's exhibits. The spaces between the exhibits were dense with trees and brush, small flower gardens, ponds, alcoves containing benches where the weary could rest. Much of it was quite lovely. Yet here and there small scenes of torture and mayhem had been created, so one could be strolling along, looking into the trees, enjoying the natural beauty of it all, then see a body hanging from a tree limb or a giant spider crouching behind bushes and such like things. Jarring, it was. Unpleasant. In the midst of life, death is ever present.

Soon I was back at the entrance with its strange bridge, no further ahead than when I had started. Now all I had to do was dart across the skull bridge and go back through the snakes.

TWO

Before returning to the dormitory, there was something I wanted to check—the garbage piled behind the kitchen. A cliche perhaps, but it's true: you can tell a lot about people by rummaging through their rubbish. And sometimes you can find out things they'd rather you didn't know. I was not keen on the idea of digging through garbage in the dead of night, what with rats and cockroaches and mice and who knows what else hiding among the refuse, but there was no avoiding it. If I was lucky, something useful might turn up as a reward for my efforts.

I used the torch to study the heap of rubbish, trying to identify the newest bags and bits. Then I started ripping open bags and examining their contents.

Most of what I found was refuse from the kitchen—mango peels, leftover curries, empty plastic water bottles, empty milk cartons, spoiled rice, wilted cabbage. There was a crumpled piece of paper, tossed into the pile on its own. I grabbed it, smoothed it out. It looked like a letter. It had coffee stains on it. With no time to read it, I put it in my pocket and kept looking. More bags, more refuse, more smelly trash. Plastic. Cardboard. Glass bottles. Cigarette butts. What a mess.

Wearing flip-flops, I tried not to think about rats and mice and what would happen if I got bitten. I hoped they would be more afraid of me than I was of them, that they would hurry off in the opposite direction when they saw me coming.

I ripped open another bag, discovered a cache of plastic water bottles and empty milk cartons, tossed it aside.

It was really quite hopeless. I could never hope to open all the bags, much less examine their contents properly—not at night, not with the limited light of the torch, not without making a huge mess that someone would notice and have to clean up. I stood up straight, easing the kink in my back, wrinkling my nose because of the foul smell. I was thinking that it would be a good idea to ask one of my fellow monks from Bangkok to come assist me, when there was a sound behind me.

Before I had a chance to turn around and see who or what was making the sound, there was a loud whack—and the back of my head exploded with sudden, sickening pain.

I fell down like a sack of potato peels and that was the end of that.

THREE

Ouch. My head. What in the world?

"Ananda? You okay?"

I opened my eyes, felt a stab of hot, angry pain, and closed them. Someone or other was hovering over me, fussing like a nursemaid.

"Ananda?"

It took me awhile to realize that Brother Kusalo was hunched over me, trying to get me to sit up, to open my eyes, to explain what was going on. At that particular moment I didn't feel much like sitting up or explaining anything. I did anyway.

"Someone hit me," I said, my voice sounding more enraged than I wanted it to. "Someone hit me!"

"What do you mean?" Kusalo asked. "What are you doing out here by yourself?"

I caught Kusalo's features in the dim light, saw that he was concerned, even a bit bewildered. He looked flustered, confused, out of sorts.

"I was looking through the trash," I confessed.

"For what?"

I shrugged.

"Can you stand?"

I got to my feet. I was a bit unsteady but very much alive and still mobile.

"Somebody hit me," I said again. I was having trouble believing it. Had I made someone uncomfortable by digging through the trash? What were they afraid I would find? Was that someone watching me, watching my movements? I glanced around, searched the shadows, but saw no one.

"I saw Silapalo, out in the parking lot, going to the Garden," Kusalo said. "It was about five minutes ago. Do you think it might have been him?"

That was a reasonable conclusion. My footsteps immediately began taking me in that direction.

"I went to your *kuti* to make sure you and your novice were okay," Kusalo continued. "But your *kuti* was empty. Then I remembered that you had gone to sleep in the dorm, so I went over there to check, saw your novice was there but not you. I guess I got a little worried. You're my responsibility, you know."

"Your responsibility?"

"Well, I'm supposed to be making sure that you have everything you need and that no one interferes with your investigation. And, well, you are a celebrity, you know—the famous Father Ananda and all that."

I tried very hard not to roll my eyes in annoyance.

"So anyway," he continued, "when I didn't see you I started poking around. I heard some noise, found you back here."

"What time is it?" I asked.

"About midnight. Why don't you let me have a look at the bump on your head—don't want you to get a concussion or anything. I'm the monastery's infirmarian, by the way—you're in good hands."

I offered a smile of appreciation. "That can wait. I want to go to the Garden."

"Now?"

"Yes, now. I want to know what Silapalo is up to."

We went to the Garden and once more I hurried through the tunnel-like entrance and across the skull bridge.

"Help me look for him," I said. "You take the right side, I'll take the left."

We made our way around the circuit, Kusalo peering into the darkness and shadows on the right side of the path, myself into the left. But we saw nothing. Not a trace of Brother Silapalo.

"Let's go check his *kuti*," I said. "Do you know which one it is?"

"Of course."

We hurried out of the Garden. My head throbbed with pain, every rush of blood making it seize up unpleasantly.

Brother Silapalo, as I recalled, was the shifty one during that day's interviews, the one who was obviously lying. What did he have to do with any of this? Was he the killer? Was he trying to get me out of the way, like he'd gotten Pandito and his sister out of the way?

I was breathless by the time we reached his *kuti*. Kusalo, with his torch in hand, went up the stairs, shined the light inside. Silapalo was lying on his mat, fast asleep—or at least pretending to be.

I walked up the steps myself, took the torch, went into Silapalo's *kuti*, shining the light in his face, calling out his name.

He rolled over, opened his eyes, seemed flabbergasted to find me standing there.

"Where have you been?" I asked.

"Been?"

"Yes. Tonight. What have you been doing?"

"I've been sleeping. What do you think I've been doing?"

"You were seen in the parking lot going to the Garden of Hell."

"But that's impossible—I haven't gone anywhere."

He got to his feet, rubbing at his eyes, looking like a monk who had just been woken up. Unlike this afternoon, his answers seemed genuine, honest.

"Why did you hit me?" I asked.

A look of confusion spread across his face.

"Why?" I demanded.

"I didn't hit you. I've done nothing. I've been right here, sleeping. What are you getting at?"

"I was out behind the kitchen and someone hit me over the head. The only one seen walking around was you. I can put two and two together."

"I haven't been anywhere."

His face was deadly earnest.

"You were lying to me today, during that interview," I said, changing course.

His eyes immediately fell away. He looked sideways, would not hold my gaze. His behavior had gone from straight forward and honest to dishonest—which led me to believe that Silapalo had been right here, sleeping, just as he said.

I questioned him further, but it was pointless. He was either a very good pretender or innocent. Figuring out which was going to prove most difficult.

FOUR

In the morning I had a nice headache—about a 7.5 on the Richter Scale. I suppose I was lucky, but I didn't feel that way. I also made a surprising discovery. I had forgotten about the letter I'd found in the trash; when I went to retrieve it from the pocket of my robe, it was gone. Whoever had hit me over the head had taken the letter—that was probably the item they didn't want me to find.

I felt a bit of regret that I hadn't thought to read it while I'd had the chance. The only thing I could remember was that it had been addressed to the abbot, and had been stained by coffee grounds.

Damn, damn, damn.

"Pho?"

Novice Jak peered down at me, perhaps wondering why I had yet to get out of bed. He already had, had been to the bathroom to do his morning routine, was ready for another day. His face was scrunched up in earnestness.

"Why don't you go ahead without me?" I suggested.

"You're not going to do the morning chants?"

"No," I said. "I'm going to lie here for a little bit. I don't feel so well."

"Are you sick?"

"I'm fine. I'll catch up with you later."

He bit his lip, knew me well enough to know that something was going on, but also knew me well enough to know not to press the matter. He left along with the others, leaving me to relish the silence.

Follow the leads . . .

I heard Pol Gen Pricha's voice in my head. *Follow the leads*—what leads? I had nothing. Notes whose handwriting didn't match that of any of the monks. A set of prayer beads. A brother and sister who had died under mysterious circumstances. Mysterious red flakes on their faces. Children who were brought in late at night for "polishing up" before being sent off to who knows where a few nights later. A letter that I hadn't read, which had been taken from me, which had coffee stains on it. Talk about how the Garden made a lot of money. A piece of a monk's robe that didn't match up to any of the monks.

It all added up to nothing concrete. No matter how I struggled to put the pieces of the puzzle together, they just wouldn't fit.

How did Silapalo fit into the picture? What motive would he have for wanting to get rid of Sister Moi and Brother Pandito? Why would he be following me around at night?

Brother Kusalo, who should have been at the morning chants with the others, came into the dormitory carrying aspirin and a bottle of water. He shook two of the aspirin out into his palm, handed them to me, handed me the water.

"Thanks," I said, grateful.

"You may go through this whole bottle before your head stops hurting," he said quietly. He adjusted his stylish black glasses, offered a youthful grin. "So how do you feel this morning?"

"Not well," I said, sitting up.

Perhaps to make sure his head was not higher than my head—a sign of disrespect—he sat down, cross-legged, continuing to look at me.

"I'm fine," I said. "Really. Just a bit of a headache. Nothing for you to worry about."

"I just want to be sure."

"It's a good thing I've got such a thick skull."

"There's going to be trouble today," he said.

"Trouble?"

"Pandito's family is furious, I heard. They want answers."

"They deserve as much."

"We don't have any answers," Kusalo pointed out.

"We know that Pandito didn't kill himself."

"Not according to the police report. When the family heard about that, they went crazy—two suicides in a month's time? Brother and sister? They're not buying it. They've threatened to go to the media if we don't come up with answers soon."

"Let them," I said.

"We don't need that kind of publicity," Kusalo said. "The abbot is afraid that tourists will stop coming."

He would be.

"Anyway," Kusalo said, "I have a feeling there's going to be a lot of fireworks today."

For that matter, so did I.

FIVE

After Kusalo left to join the others, I grabbed my monk's bag and rummaged inside it, looking for the business cards that I had taken from Pandito's *kuti* the day before, which I had yet to look at.

I was getting sloppy that way—out of practice, as it were, flying by the seat of my orange robes. Having been a monk for almost nine years, I was not in the habit of hurrying and found it much too easy to forget things. If I wanted to figure out what was going on at Wat Yai, though, I was going to have to try harder and stop being so lackadaisical. Just like last night—I should have read that letter while I was standing there. Why hadn't I? I gave myself an inward kick in the seat of the pants for being so disorganized.

Pandito's business cards were mostly from businessmen: a man who worked at a concrete factory, a computer distributor, a mobile phone salesman, an insurance salesman. Pandito, as the tour guide for the Garden of Hell, had no doubt met a great many people who couldn't resist the temptation to pull out a business card and introduce themselves—networking, it was called, if I remembered correctly.

One card interested me a great deal: It was a card from a NGO group devoted to stamping out human trafficking called STOP, or Stop Trafficking of Persons. The contact listed on the card was a Thai woman; her office was located in Bangkok.

Why would Pandito have such a card in his possession? Or wasn't that rather obvious?

SIX

Brother Kittisaro called from Bangkok shortly after breakfast.

"What did you find?" I asked straight off.

I could picture Kittisaro sitting at his receptionist's desk in the abbot's office, a man in charge of three computer screens and all of Wat Mahanat's paperwork, finances, and goings-on. I could see his wire frame glasses and delicate features while he "surfed" the Internet or updated some database or other. Kittisaro and I had taken the robes at about the same time, and over the years we had grown very close.

"What I didn't find is more interesting," Kittisaro said, a hint of mystery in his voice.

"What didn't you find?"

"There's no record of Wat Yai having anything to do with processing refugee children—I even talked to the Immigration Department, just to be sure. They have no record of Wat Yai performing any such service as you described to me."

"What else?"

"Not much, Ananda. Of course it's well known that the abbot's brother is a mafia godfather in that part of the country—you'd better watch your step."

"You're telling me."

"Why do you say that?"

"I got beat on the head last night while I was looking through their trash."

"Ouch."

"That's what I said."

"So they already know you're digging around?"

"Of course they do. They knew that the first day I got here."

"Well, just be careful—some of us over here worry about you, you know."

"I know."

"I don't get the connection, though," he said.

"Connection?"

"Yes. Between the brother and sister, and this refugee program."

"I'm thinking of motive," I said. "I'm thinking that maybe the brother and sister cottoned on to what was going on with the refugee program and maybe got themselves whacked because they threatened to spill the beans. Aside from that, I can't come up with any motive as to why either of them was killed."

"I see," Kittisaro said. "That would be a powerful motive, wouldn't it—exposing wrongdoing?"

Yes. Especially when there were large amounts of cash involved.

SEVEN

Brother Kusalo was in the open-air *sala* with Abbot Uddi when Jak and I approached. I asked Jak to wait for me as I mounted the steps to the *sala*.

"Father Ananda," Abbot Uddi said, in greeting.

"Reverend Father," I replied, giving him the respect his office deserved. "I should like to know more about the refugee children—I'd like to see some of the paperwork, in fact—if you don't mind."

"What does that have to do with anything?"

I shrugged, said nothing, as if the matter wasn't really of much consequence, just some routine thing that needed doing.

"Brother Kusalo can show you the paperwork," the abbot said, waving a dismissive hand at Kusalo. "He knows where all the files are."

"Thank you," I replied.

Kusalo led Jak and myself to the abbot's office.

"What exactly do you want to see?" Kusalo asked.

"The usual—the license, the records. Whatever you have."

He pointed to a certificate mounted on the wall above the filing cabinets. "That's the license. It's good for three years. I'll get the books."

While he did that, I studied the license, which looked official enough. It had been issued by the Immigration Department, was due to expire next year.

Of itself, the license didn't mean much. With today's computers and printers, you could produce almost any sort of document, including passports and marriage licenses, that were virtually identical to the real thing.

I jotted down the license number on a pad of paper—that was at least one thing I could double-check.

Kusalo proceeded to show me ledgers that documented the arrival and departure of the children, most of whom were refugees, a few of whom were runaways who needed to be reunited with their parents. The records included arrival and departure dates for each "batch." Each "batch" listed the names of the children—if only their first names—and where they had been sent.

I made notes on my pad.

"Everything's above board," Kusalo said. He seemed a bit surprised that I would take any interest in the matter.

"I'm not so sure of that," I said.

"Why not?"

I gave him a long look, wondering how much I could trust this man. How close was he to the abbot? How much did he know about what was going on in this place? Was he a player or a wide-eyed, clueless innocent?

My instinct pegged him as an innocent—he was little more than the handsome face sent out to greet the faithful, the intelligent one who did the books and didn't think to ask too many questions. I took a gamble. "It seems the Immigration Department doesn't know about your operation here. I wonder how that could be—that they have no record of it."

"We have our license," he protested. "There must be some mistake—some confusion."

"It won't hurt to double-check," I said.

"Double-check? But why?"

"Do you know much about human trafficking?" I asked.

His face said he did not. He did not even answer my question.

"Women and children are routinely trafficked," I said. "They're sold to brothels in China or Japan or elsewhere. They might even be sold to our own brothels right here in Thailand. They're also sold off as maids, waitresses, who knows. That's why it concerns me that the Immigration Department doesn't have any records concerning your operations—are you sure these kids are being sent to refugee camps?"

"Of course they are," he said. "Where else would they be sent?"

"Brothels," I said.

"For what?"

Was he really that innocent, that naive? Or was he truly surprised by my line of questioning?

"What do you think they do in brothels?" I asked.

"Not with children."

I held my tongue.

"I can assure you that there's nothing like that going on here," Kusalo said, as if the very thought offended him. "We process these kids as a service to the community, not to sell them to brothels. Even the idea is ridiculous."

"Be that as it may," I said. "It won't hurt to check it out."

"You go right ahead," he said. "But I don't see what it has to do with Pandito's death."

"I'm thinking about motive," I said.

"Motive?"

"Yes. As in why would anyone want to kill Moi and her brother Pandito? Perhaps they knew something and someone wanted them silenced. I didn't even get a chance to talk to Pandito—he was killed almost as soon as I got here. I'm thinking his sister might have told him something, something that got her killed. When I showed up, perhaps they thought it was better to silence Pandito too, before he had a chance to spill the beans."

"Oh."

Indeed.

"Who killed them?" he asked.

"That's what we have to try to figure out."

"There's no reason why anyone here would want to kill them—this is a monastery, you know, not the big city."

"This is a monastery that makes a lot of money," I pointed out. "And when people are making money, trouble always follows."

EIGHT

Brother Pabhassaro—the monk who had found Sister Moi's body almost a month ago now, and the only monk I had not yet interviewed—was a big man with an unfriendly face and a sour disposition. I discovered this when Kusalo led Jak and myself across the grounds, to the Garden, and into the back of the Garden where Brother Pabhassaro had his office and the tools of his trade—he was the maintenance man for the Garden, was responsible for the feeding and watering of the crocodiles and other animals, was responsible for keeping fences mended and the Garden clean.

"This is Father Ananda," Kusalo said, introducing me.

"I know who he is," Pabhassaro snapped.

"He would like to talk to you about Sister Moi," Kusalo said.

"What's there to talk about?"

"I'd like to talk about the morning you discovered her body," I said.

"Like I said," he replied, "what's there to talk about? The idiot woman threw herself into the croc enclosure. Was a terrible mess to clean up after, I can tell you that. Getting her body out of there wasn't easy."

"Do you remember anything strange about that morning, anything that might explain why she would have wanted to kill herself?"

"All I found was her body. No suicide note, if that's what you mean."

"Was it a suicide," I asked, "or perhaps something else?"

"What else could it be?" Pabhassaro asked, squinting at me as if I were a demon dressed in orange robes.

"I'm not so sure it was suicide," I said. "I'm not sure at all."

"Wouldn't surprise me," Pabhassaro said. "She got on your nerves, she did. She was always complaining about them—those crocs—complaining that they were getting too big, were too expensive to maintain. Like it was any of her business."

"She didn't like the crocodiles?"

"Thought they were dangerous—she was afraid they were going to get out, were going to hurt someone. That woman was always going on about something or other."

"Do you have any idea why someone might have wanted to kill her?"

"Plenty—she was meddlesome. She should have learned how to keep her mouth shut and stay out of other people's business. She was just a nun, after all. Had no call to be so nosy."

"You don't kill someone just because they're nosy," I pointed out.

"If they're nosy enough, you just might," Pabhassaro replied.

I paused, gave him a long stare. He stared back at me, unflinching. His dislike for the woman was obvious, but that didn't mean he killed her. Yet, as maintenance man for the Garden, who better to kill her? And Pandito too, since Pandito's body was discovered in the Garden? And both Moi and Pandito had argued with him.

"Seems like you ought to be talking to Brother Panya," Pabhassaro said. "She accused him of raping her—if I was him, I might have strangled her, if only for that reason alone."

Hmm.

"How much money does this place make?" I asked, changing the subject.

"You'd have to ask the folks in the office. I have no idea. I'm the maintenance man, not an accountant."

"You've never had any problem trying to feed all these animals?"

"Nope."

"What do you feed them?"

"Chickens. Pig guts. Mangoes. You name it, they'll eat it."

"Is that right? What about Brother Pandito—any idea how his body came to be hanging from one of your exhibits?"

"Haven't got the slightest idea. He was another one."

"Another what?"

"Meddlesome—always telling me how to run my business. Couldn't be bothered to help out—to do something, I mean, really do something, except be a tour guide. All sorts of advice that man had, but not a lick of sense. He had a dozen exhibits he wanted to add to the Garden, but he had no idea how difficult they are to construct."

"Why do you think he hanged himself in your Garden?"

"It's not *my* Garden. And who knows why he hanged himself, if that's what you think he did."

"What did he do?"

"He got himself killed," Pabhassaro avowed.

"How do you know that?"

"That's the gossip. That's what everyone's saying."

"Do you have any idea as to who might have killed him?"

"How should I know? I'm not the police. Now, if you don't mind, I've got work to do."

"Well, one more thing. I need to check your robes—I'll need you to get your spare set."

"What for?"

"I'd rather not say."

He made an unhappy face. He removed his outer robe, allowed me to look at it. I was hoping to find a telltale patch of cloth missing, but no. The robe was clean. I looked at the others. I waited until he brought his spare set. But to no avail.

I bit my lip in frustration.

NINE

"Not a very friendly man," I said.

"No, he's not," Kusalo agreed. "I'm surprised he didn't tell you."

"Tell me what?"

"He and Sister Moi had a big argument just a day or two before she died."

"About what?"

"The Garden. Sister Moi believed that female mannequins were 'degrading' to women, that they should be redone—she said they were too 'sexy.' She had a point."

She did indeed.

"Her and Pabhassaro argued about it?"

"Apparently. Sister Moi had removed one of the mannequins from a display and Pabhassaro got angry with her because she didn't have permission to be tearing up the displays. They got into a yelling match out in the parking lot, and neither one of them was about to back down."

I considered that silently. Was it motive enough for murder? Was it the proverbial straw that broke the camel's back, the final little annoyance that pushed Pabhassaro over the edge? Murders have been committed over far more trivial matters.

TEN

As we crossed the parking lot, Pandito's mother caught sight of me and headed in my direction. I steeled myself for a confrontation—the look on her face said it wasn't going to be pleasant. Not pleasant at all.

Unsurprisingly, it wasn't.

"You!" she exclaimed, coming to stand right in front of me, staring up at me with pained, reddened eyes. "This is your fault!" She pointed an angry finger at my face.

Her son, trailing along behind her, took her arm and tried to calm her down. "Mae," he said gently. *Mother*.

"I will not be quiet!" she snapped. "The abbot said there would be trouble if people came poking around, and he was right! What did you come here for? Wasn't my daughter enough? Now my son too? Are you happy now, Mr. Big Shot Monk from the Big City?"

I was speechless.

"Mae," the son said again, trying to take his mother's arm. "This is no good." *Mai dee*. No good.

And it wasn't: Arguing or getting physical with a monk was highly disrespectful. But at that moment, I wasn't thinking of my own dignity so much as the rage and pain this woman must be feeling over the loss of her son and daughter. "I'm sorry," I managed to say.

"That's not good enough!" she exclaimed loudly. "I want my son back. Can you bring my son back, you Big Shot Monk from the Big City? Can you do that? Why did you have to stir up trouble? Why couldn't you have just left things alone? What's to become of me?"

Some of the monks of Wat Yai converged on the scene, separating us—but not before Pandito's mother had the chance to slap me full across the face. The blow stung. I was surprised at its swiftness. Then Pandito's mother was escorted away and I was left to stand with Novice Jak and Brother Kusalo, embarrassed and out of sorts.

"That's not right," Kusalo said. "She doesn't know what she's saying."

Trouble was, though, she did. And she was right: My coming to Wat Yai had cost her the life of one of her sons. It hadn't been intentional, of course, but the result was the same.

ELEVEN

After a phone call to Kittisaro in Bangkok, Jak and I walked into the village and found ourselves a taxi—we had to wait about forty minutes before one finally showed up.

"We'd like to go to Wat Damri," I told the driver.

"Why are we going there, Pho?" Jak wanted to know.

"Going to check something out," I said.

"What?"

"Something."

"What? I can't help you if you don't tell me what we're doing."

"I don't need you to help me."

He made a face, frowned, turned to look out the window.

Feeling bad—I didn't want to exclude him but also didn't want him to come to harm—I said, "Oh, all right. We're going to Wat Damri because they have a refugee resettlement program."

"Like Wat Yai?" he asked, his eyes brightening.

"Yes," I said. "Exactly like Wat Yai. I just want to go have a look."

"Why?"

"I don't know. A hunch, maybe."

That wasn't quite true. On the phone with Kittisaro, I had learned that the license number being used at Wat Yai was the same one that had been issued to the nearby Wat Damri. And I thought I knew why.

Miles of countryside went by. The sight of the endless rice fields and banana plantations and palm trees was relaxing—the earth's beauty never failed to impress me. But it also made me wonder why we humans could make it so ugly with our concrete and wire and steel and progress and development. And where was all this progress leading anyway? I, for one, had no clue. It certainly wasn't making people happier, not if my experience was anything to go by. It seemed to be making everyone greedier and more unhappy as time went by.

Wat Damri was about thirty minutes away, located in the midst of a small village called Roi. Once we arrived at the temple's gates, I asked the taxi driver to wait for us so that he could double his fare by taking us back to Wat Yai. Jak and I got out, stretched our legs, went in search of the abbot.

We found him in the main office.

"Father Ananda!" he exclaimed. He seemed happy to see us.

"Reverend Father," I replied.

"Surprised to see you here," the abbot said. "We don't get many celebrities passing through Roi."

No, they probably didn't.

"What can I do for you?" he asked. He was a sturdy man, a bit plump. He had a smile ever at the ready. I decided that I liked him.

"I would like to know more about your refugee resettlement program," I said. "Would it be possible for me to see your license, the records?"

"But of course," the abbot said happily.

He led Jak and myself into his private office.

"The license," he said, pointing to one of the framed pictures on the wall.

I looked at it, noted the similarities with the one in Abbot Uddi's office. In fact, they looked exactly alike, as if a photocopy had been made. Only this certificate had gold embossing, whereas the one at Wat Yai did not.

In other words, the abbot at Wat Yai had gotten his hands on a certificate like this—perhaps this very one, since it bore the same license number—and had made a copy of it, whiting out the name of Wat Damri and putting in the name of Wat Yai.

The abbot then showed me the books: Records at Wat Damri were much more extensive and well kept. The files contained pictures and fingerprints of the children along with their full names and nationalities, where they had been before arriving at Wat Damri, where they were to be sent afterward. The destinations were much the same as the ones given to me by Abbot Uddi.

"Is it possible to see the children?" I asked.

"I'd be happy to show you," the abbot replied.

He led us outside into the temple complex. It was just as sprawling and nonchalant as Wat Yai, buildings thrown up here and there in no particular order, a school on one side of the property, a small market on the other side, a grove of trees in back housing dozens of *kuti*. Dogs snoozed here and there in shady, sandy spots. Younger monks swept the grounds, gave us curious glances.

Unlike Wat Yai, the resettlement program here was part of the temple complex itself, located in a small three-story building that had been built specifically to house it, according to the abbot. There were about twenty children playing outside this building and they greeted the abbot with *wai* gestures of respect, but also with playful smiles, as if the abbot was a man they liked and admired—and also, I thought, as if they had been here long enough to get to know the man.

Inside we found monks going about their business—cleaning, cooking, making beds, tending to paperwork, sweeping up dorm rooms, mopping floors.

"How does the program work?" I asked the abbot.

"We receive the children from Bangkok," he answered, "and then we process them—all the paperwork has to be just so—you know how bureaucrats are about their paperwork."

"How long do the children stay?"

"Depends," the abbot said. "Usually about a month or two, but sometimes longer, especially if we have trouble tracking down documents or verifying their nationality. And not all these children are refugees. Many are Thai—they've been orphaned for one reason or another. Parents died of AIDS, that sort of thing—you know how it is. We hold them here until we can find a place for them at an orphanage."

He explained that perhaps a dozen children arrived at the center each month while another dozen were sent off, their paperwork in order, their destinations finally decided upon. This was nothing like the numbers of children going through Wat Yai. The entire atmosphere was different. The children here seemed happy, at peace, as if they were being treated well. And unlike Wat Yai, there were just as many boys as girls, ranging in age from two all the way to seventeen. That fact alone was especially telling.

What I saw troubled me because it could only mean one thing: the children being "processed" at Wat Yai were not refugees on their way to refugee camps. They were being trafficked. And if that was so—and I believed it was—then I was in a heck of a spot, because the only way for Wat Yai to run a business of that sort would be with help from the local godfather—Abbot Uddi's brother. If the mafia were involved, threatening their interests could be deadly. It would be all too easy to kill an interfering monk or two rather than to let their trafficking ring come under scrutiny by the authorities.

"May I ask why you're interested in our program?" the abbot asked.

"Just curiosity," I said. "It seems to me that you do some very good work here. The children seem to be fine."

"Only problem is, the children have to leave—we *do* get attached. Attachments are not good, but they're just children, after all, and many of them have no parents. We'd like to just keep them all and let them grow up here, but of course we don't have the facilities for that."

Should I ask the abbot about his license number—should I share with him the information that Wat Yai was using a copy of his license? I wanted to, but did not dare. It would not do for this abbot to start asking questions—at least not just yet.

"You've been very helpful," I said.

"Really?" He seemed amazed.

"Yes, indeed you have been. We appreciate your time."

"Not a problem."

We returned to the taxi and said our goodbyes.

TWELVE

On our way back to Wat Yai, I asked the cab driver to take us to see the family of Panya and Subha. That was another matter that I wanted to follow up on.

The taxi driver took us down a small dirt road, past farms and orchards. The farmhouse where the family of Panya and Subha lived was much like that of Pandito's family.

An old woman came to the door of the Thai-style house, up on stilts, and looked down at us.

I went forward a few steps, but waited, not wanting to intrude or force myself upon the woman.

She came down the stairs slowly and walked over to where I stood, but keeping a discreet distance. "May I help you, Father?"

I explained who I was, that I had once been a police officer and was investigating the goings-on at Wat Yai. I asked her if she knew that one of her sons had been accused of raping Sister Moi.

She glared at me with hateful eyes. "You're just like all the rest, aren't you?"

"In what way?"

"Believing that nonsense," she said. "The way that nun carried on, pretending to be so innocent—what a sham!"

I bit at my lower lip. This was certainly a new twist. "What do you mean, exactly?" I asked.

She gave me a long look as if to see whether I was really interested, or was just humoring her.

"I've only heard one side of the story," I said. "I would appreciate it if you would tell me the other."

"Well, then, if that's how it is . . . that nun, that Sister Moi . . . she was a piece of work. She knew that my son Panya went to the Garden on some nights to meditate, and she followed him, throwing herself at him like a harlot, exposing herself, carrying on like a school girl with a crush. And Panya always had a hard time with girls. I mean, he liked them too much. It was the hardest thing in the world for him to follow his brother into the religious life, and he was getting along fine until that Sister Moi came along and started tormenting him. Well, my son realized he wasn't cut out for the robes, and he asked this woman to marry him, to go away with him, to leave the religious life. They would get married, do things properly, have a family, settle down. And she went along with it. She agreed. They were in love."

This was definitely not the story I had heard.

"Anyway," she said, "that girl came up pregnant, and it wasn't my son's doing. The abbot demanded to see her, demanded that she explain herself. She and Panya had agreed they would come clean, confess their intentions to the abbot, ask to leave the robes, and all that. He didn't know whose baby she was carrying, but he was going to do right by her anyway, and help her out. But instead, she went to see the abbot and accused Panya of raping her. Rape! What was she thinking? She was the one who kept sending him notes, asking him to meet her in the Garden. Who knows which of the other monks she was fooling around with? Then suddenly she plays innocent, like she doesn't know anything about sex, and she accuses my son of raping her.

"My son came to see me, to explain all of this. I was furious. I told him to get his brother to provide an alibi—if she was going to lie, my son was going to have to protect himself. So it came down to her word against my sons'. Then she killed herself. Of course, I was glad of that, glad to be rid of her. But now my sons are being talked about, still being accused of getting her pregnant, for killing her, for who knows what else."

"So your son wasn't the father of her baby?" I asked.

"Of course not," she said. "He knew the rules of the monastery. He knew that having sex would mean he was defeated. He didn't want that. If he was going to leave the monastery, he would do it properly, be a gentleman, wait until they were married."

I tried to wrap my mind around this unexpected information. If Sister Moi was not who she pretended to be, and if she had been enticing monks and toying with their affections, she might have made one of them angry enough to kill her—especially if she came up pregnant with another man's child.

I thanked the woman for her time and left.

CHAPTER FIVE

*"Failure is the faithful companion of the sage.
No other mentor is as wise or true."*
—*The Sage's Tao Te Ching: A New Interpretation*, #79

ONE

After lunch I called Khun Nida, the woman listed on the business card I had taken from Brother Pandito's cell. Nida was in charge of the STOP project.

"What can I do for you, Father Ananda?" Her voice was bright, pleasant, assured.

I explained who I was, how I had come into possession of her name and phone number. "Did you know Brother Pandito?"

"Briefly," she said, adding no more than that.

"Did he contact you?"

"Yes, he did. Can I ask what this is about?"

"Brother Pandito is dead, I'm afraid. I'm trying to figure out what happened to him. I think he might have stumbled onto something that got him killed."

There was a long pause on the other side of the phone. She cleared her throat. "And what do you want from me?"

"I was hoping you might tell me what you and Pandito discussed."

"He wanted to know about child trafficking, so I gave him the usual spiel—lots of people call and ask."

"Did he express any concerns to you about Wat Yai—about a refugee resettlement program?"

"Yes, he did. He said the temple there was running some sort of program but he wasn't sure what exactly it was. He was suspicious."

"How long ago did he contact you?"

"He visited me a couple of weeks ago. He said he'd come to Bangkok to take care of some family business, asked if I might spare him some time."

"Did he tell you anything specific about Wat Yai, his suspicions, anything like that?"

"Not really," she replied. "He said he would go back and look into the matter a bit further, then get back to me. But he never did. Do you think he got himself into trouble?"

"I'm almost sure of it," I replied. "Deadly trouble."

"That's the nature of the business," she said. "You have to be careful with these people—no telling what they might do. I've lost track of the number of death threats we've received here. Mostly from mafia types who think they can do whatever they please."

"They *can* do whatever they please," I pointed out.

"And so can the rest of us," she said.

TWO

"How would you like a big story?" I asked.

Jenjira, a reporter for *Thai Rath*, the country's best-selling daily newspaper, was on the other end of the phone line. "I'm all ears," she said.

"What if I told you that I knew of a temple that was part of a human trafficking ring?"

"I'd say, what else is new?"

"Don't be so jaded."

"Hard not to, Father Ananda. You monks get up to the most atrocious things. Nothing surprises me anymore, not about monks and temples."

"We're all human," I said.

"Too much so, from what I've seen."

Ouch.

She was right—monks did get up to the most unholy of things.

"I'm not sure how I should deal with the situation," I said. "If I spill the beans, I could get hurt. But if you spill the beans, maybe something will get done."

"So we're not just talking theoretically here?"

"No."

"You've got a temple running a trafficking ring?"

"Taking part in it, at least. It seems the temple serves as a way station for kids being trafficked. I don't know where they're coming from or where they're going. The license being used is the same license for a legitimate program at another temple. It must have been copied, doctored up with a computer or something. And we've got monks and nuns dying over here."

"Are you at Wat Yai?"

"How did you know?"

"There was a nun there who killed herself by jumping into the crocodile pit, from what I heard."

"I don't think she killed herself. I think she was pushed."

"Now there's a story, Father."

"You're not kidding. And now a monk has come up dead under suspicious circumstances—and he just happens to be the nun's real-life brother."

"I'm listening."

"I think he was killed because I was sent here to investigate—I think he might have known something and they wanted him silenced. And he was. Before I had a chance to talk to him."

"And what do you want from me?"

"Help," I said. "If you run a story on it, the heat will be on—everyone and their mother will be looking at Wat Yai with a fine-toothed comb. If that happens, I might be able to shake loose a few things and get to the bottom of who killed the brother and sister."

"It's dangerous," she said. "Are you absolutely sure of your facts?"

"I'm sure," I said. I explained about the license, how I had visited Wat Damri, all the differences I had noticed in the record-keeping and the general atmosphere of the two programs, especially the differences on the children's faces and in their behavior.

"But if the mafia is involved, you can bet the local authorities are involved too," she pointed out. "They may do a half-assed investigation, and in a week or two everyone will forget about it—and then where will you be?"

She was speaking of our unfortunate propensity to forget things almost as soon as they happen. Living in the moment has its disadvantages. Even the most heinous of crimes played up to no end in the media disappear off the public radar with astonishing swiftness.

"Can't be helped," I said. "It might give me enough time to get to the bottom of things."

"I can be there later on this afternoon—what is it, a three-hour drive?"

"About that," I said. "I'll watch for you."

"Bye then."

She rang off.

THREE

"Where are we going, Pho?" Jak wanted to know.

"Need to see Lt Poom," I replied.

We were walking on the dusty road that led into the village. The hitch in Jak's step was more noticeable today—we'd been doing rather a lot of walking lately. I felt sorry for him but said nothing, not wanting to draw attention to his bad leg.

"Wouldn't it be nice to live in a place like this?" I asked, feeling him out on the subject.

"Oh please," he replied, drawing out the "please" in an exaggerated fashion. "You'd die of boredom in no time flat."

"Nothing wrong with peace and quiet."

"For you, maybe. I mean, there's nothing to do here except play with buffaloes. It's so boring!"

I glanced at him, saw how he scrunched up his face as if to physically suggest how distasteful the thought of living in the country was to him.

I needed to discuss with him the possibility of moving to a temple in the countryside—I needed to know how he felt about it. I already knew, though, didn't I? And he had just confirmed it: he would not want to leave Bangkok.

"What if I said that I was thinking about asking to transfer to another temple?" I said, giving him a sideways glance.

"Really?"

"Yes."

"You want to transfer somewhere else?"

I nodded.

He frowned, turned his eyes away from me, trained them on the ground in front of us.

Our temple in Bangkok, Wat Mahanat, was home. His home. Or at least the only home he really knew, now that his parents were dead and he had no relatives willing to care for him. He had a history there, roots, friends, a life. For a child who had already lost so much, it would be impossible to ask him to give up what little he had left.

"You want to leave Wat Mahanat?" he asked.

"No," I said. "But I may have to. You remember Police Major General Chao and his thugs?"

He nodded. How could he forget? It was Chao and his men that we had run afoul of while trying to figure out the murder of one of the youths in our homeless program last year. During the course of that investigation, I had discovered that Chao had four men posing as monks at our monastery and was using them to run drugs in the city. Not to mention the fact that the men were wanted by authorities for drug-related crimes.

"Chao's been sending me some love letters," I said. "He's made his intentions pretty clear. He's not happy with the way I embarrassed him, the way he lost face—in fact, he's quite angry about it and keeps vowing to do something to even the score. If I remain at Wat Mahanat, well, who knows what will happen."

"So you have to leave?"

"It's starting to look that way," I replied. "The abbot has been pressuring me to leave—he doesn't want any more trouble."

"So why don't you leave?"

"Because I don't know what to do about you."

He pursed his lips, said nothing. A look of worry spread across his face.

"You could stay, if you wanted to," I pointed out.

That made him frown even more deeply.

"We have to start thinking about what we're going to do," I said. "We're going to have to make a decision."

He remained silent. Instead of walking beside me, he slowed his pace and was soon behind me—perhaps he didn't want me to see his face. I glanced backward, saw him biting his lip, studiously avoiding my eyes.

FOUR

Jak sat outside while I went into Lt Poom's office. I sat down in the chair opposite his desk.

"How is everything out at Wat Yai?" he asked.

"That's why I'm here," I said. "What do you know about Wat Yai and human trafficking?"

He winced, looked away, licked his lips.

He knew.

"Question is," I said, "what are we going to do about it?"

"What do you mean? There's nothing you can do about it."

"Not true," I said. "There's plenty I can do about it. But I need to know what I'm getting into."

"Father Ananda, this is connected all the way up the chain—and I don't think it's a good idea to be rattling this particular chain. Not if you want to live."

"I understand," I said, "but what about those children? Are you going to sit back in silence while they are sent out to brothels and who knows what else?"

He shrugged helplessly, as if his hands were tied.

"I have to do something," I said. "I can't keep silent."

"Then don't tell me anything," he replied. "I don't want to know. Just go your way and do what you've got to do and leave me out of it."

"I'll need your help," I said.

"I can't, Father Ananda. No way. I've got a wife and kids to look after. You'll have to find somebody else."

I could tell by the look on his face that he was not about to change his mind—no amount of prodding from me was going to make any difference.

"Tell me how it's connected," I said. "Who's at the top of the chain?"

He shook his head.

"Please?"

He again shook his head.

"No one will ever know it was you," I said. "You won't have to be involved at all."

"Ananda, you don't know what you're asking, what you're getting yourself into. For your sake, just drop it. Trust me: You do not want to know where this leads."

"Yes I do," I said. "Is it Mr. A?"

Mr. A was Alongkon Phongwut, the mafia boss for this province, the abbot's brother. Rather than naming him directly, the press always referred to him as Mr. A, allowing themselves a convenient escape hatch should he decide to sue for defamation of character. They could always claim they were referring to someone else. This same indirectness was also part of our parliamentary life—when someone in parliament was accused of corruption or wrong-doing, his name was never mentioned, only the first letter of his name. Pamphlets often circulated accusing "S" or "T" or "R" of this, that or the other thing. Trying to guess who was being referred to was part of the fun of politics.

"Is it?" I pressed.

"I'm not saying," Poom answered, but the way he said it meant yes, we were talking about Mr. A.

Mr. A was rumored to have friends in the current cabinet, and was also connected with some well-known military generals and police chiefs. Of course it was up to the cabinet and generals and police to control human trafficking—to stop it, in fact—but for the most part, they turned a blind eye and accepted kickbacks to continue turning that blind eye so that this despicable business could continue. Getting women and children in and out of the country required the cooperation of police and immigration officials, at the very least. There would be no human trafficking if the police and immigration officials did their jobs properly. Paid as little as they were—I should know, I used to be a police officer—it was far too tempting to accept the bribes and turn a blind eye. Few there were who would be willing to put their money where their mouth was, who would be willing to turn down free wads of cash in exchange for doing what was right and proper and decent. It was much easier to just go along with the system and try not to think too much about the consequences.

"Just leave it alone," Poom said. "For your own sake. Just let it go."

Problem was, I was stubborn about certain things, and if I got my back up, I would not stand down. And my back was up.

FIVE

We returned to Wat Yai and I went to the abbot's office in search of Brother Kusalo. We found him in the office answering the telephone. When his conversation was finished, I asked if I might be able to look in the files for awhile.

"Sure," he said. "What are you looking for?"

"Nothing in particular," I said, "I'm just hoping that something will jump out at me."

This time I started in the A's, determined to work my way from first to last, no matter how much time it would require. There was something in the files I had missed—or so a gut instinct told me. Something rather significant. And it had occurred to me that the first time I had gone through the files, Kusalo had helped me, had done the first half, and I hadn't reviewed his work. I wanted to do that now, but without arousing his animosity. He was trying to be helpful and I needed him to continue being so.

I took the first file and opened it, scanned its contents, paying special attention to the application form handwritten by the applicant-monk himself. I still had the notes—*Garden 10 pm*. I was fairly certain I could spot the handwriting if I saw it again and Kusalo might have missed it that day when we went through the files together.

File after file, I scanned, compared handwriting, looked at pictures, read reports. The files had nothing new to say to me, nothing that jumped out, nothing of significance. Were my police skills too rusty? Was I out of practice, missing the obvious? I soldiered on, perplexed, frustrated, hopeful, all at the same time.

By the time I got to the end of the files, my feet were killing me and Novice Jak had wandered off to join the other novices.

"Well?" Kusalo asked, giving me a hopeful look.

I frowned, letting my irritation show.

"What do you know about this refugee program?" I asked.

"It's been going on for about two years," he said with a shrug. "It's all pretty straightforward."

"Are you sure about that?"

"Why shouldn't I be?"

"What if I said your license was fake—that the license number was issued for Wat Damri, not Wat Yai? What would you say to that?"

"I'd say you were kidding."

"But I'm not kidding. It's a fake license—it could have been copied off a computer or something. Wat Yai doesn't have permission from the Immigration Department to be running any resettlement programs or efforts along those lines."

"Really?"

"Really. And that leads me to wonder what's going on with those kids—where are they really being sent? What's really going on here? Do you know?"

"They're sent to border camps, or repatriated to their own countries," Kusalo said defensively.

"Then why does the temple have a bogus license?"

He took a depth breath, gave me a look of sincere consternation.

"How much do you know about the trafficking of women and children?" I asked.

"Is that what you think they're doing?"

"That's what the evidence suggests," I said.

"But that's ridiculous. This is a temple, Father Ananda."

"Even so."

He continued to look bewildered. "That can't be," he said at last, caught in the grip of denial. "That just can't be. You must be mistaken."

"I don't think so."

"But this is a temple!"

Was he really so naive? Didn't he know that corruption was prevalent in all levels of society, that even monks were not immune? Didn't he know about all the scandals involving monks and temples? Sexual scandals? Drug scandals? Embezzlement scandals? Abbots who drove around in BMWs? Monks who donned wigs and went out at night to karaoke bars? Monks who killed other monks over money or passion or some combination of the two? Didn't he know police would accept bribes to look the other way, no matter what crime had been committed? That murderers could walk free as long as they had enough cash to grease the right hands? That judges could be bought or killed? That witnesses could be scared into silence? That accusers could suddenly forget their accusations and drop charges at the drop of a dime—or, more likely, a fistful of banknotes?

"That just can't be true," he said again. "It just can't be."

"Did you know the abbot's brother is rumored to be a mafia higher-up?"

"Yes, but that's not the abbot's fault. The abbot is a good man, regardless of what his brother does."

"That may or may not be true. How well do you know the abbot?"

"I've been working with him for four years now. I've never had any reason to suspect him of anything."

"Nothing ever struck you as strange, or odd, or unusual?"

He shook his head.

"Can I count on you to help me?" I asked.

"Help you to do what?"

"Figure out what's going on with these kids—and put a stop to it, if it's what I think it is."

"How are we supposed to do that?"

"I have a reporter from *Thai Rath* on the way. She'll start asking questions, snoop around, have a story in the paper tomorrow. That should be enough to get things rolling. If there is something going on, it will be exposed quickly enough, especially if it's on the front pages of *Thai Rath*."

"You called a reporter?" He seemed flabbergasted.

"Power of the press and all that," I replied. "She's an old friend."

"If you accuse the abbot of being involved in a trafficking ring—well, that will certainly stir things up. He'll be furious."

"I'm not accusing anyone of anything. I just want to know why the license you have is bogus, that's all. Maybe it's just a simple mistake that can be easily rectified. I think I'm well within my rights, as a representative of the Maha Thera Samakhom, to bring it up."

"Of course," Kusalo said. "It's just that the abbot's not going to take too kindly to your sticking your nose in his business."

"If he has nothing to hide, he has nothing to fear."

"That may be so, but he's still not going to like it."

There was a pause in the conversation. Kusalo fidgeted nervously, as if he expected hordes of mafia types to appear out of the woodwork. His voice became a breathy whisper. "Are you sure?" he asked.

"No," I replied. "But the abbot needs to explain about the license. If it's a mistake, it needs to be cleared up, and that will be that."

"What if it isn't a mistake?"

SIX

Jenjira arrived with an entourage in the afternoon and immediately got to work. She had three personal assistants, and two photographers and one man with a video camera—enough of a media presence to be somewhat formidable, if not downright frightening. The first thing she did was interview the abbot and inquire about the license for the refugee program, letting it be known that rumors were going around that it was fake.

Cars began to arrive in the late afternoon for that evening's funeral chants for Brother Pandito. I wanted to attend the chants, but did not dare, given that Pandito's mother blamed me for her son's death. Jak went along with the other novices and I walked about the grounds, trying to puzzle out in my head what was going on at this strange, dark monastery out in the middle of nowhere.

It seemed clear to me that Pandito and Moi had been silenced, that somehow or other they had discovered the truth about the refugee resettlement program and had paid for it with their lives. But who had killed them? I had my suspicions but how could I get proof? And for that matter, how far were they willing to go to keep their secret? Would they kill me too if given a chance? Was it worth the risk?

Of all the Buddhist teachings, the one concerning compassion is perhaps most fundamental. Realizing that other beings suffer just as we do should lead us to feel sorry for others, to view others with compassion, to forgive and forget and overlook mistakes and errors and all the twists and turns of human behavior. Compassion also demands that we try to help when a need is clearly expressed, when we have the opportunity to do some good for the world.

In other words, compassion demanded that I take my chances. The need of the children involved in the trafficking ring was greater than my own need for survival.

SEVEN

It was almost dark. With nothing better to do, I went to the Garden, wanting to have another look around, to see if I might have missed something or other. What, I did not know. I had the feeling that the answers I needed were all around me, but I just wasn't seeing them, wasn't paying enough attention.

I hurried through the entrance to the Garden with its trees and snakes. I scurried across the skull bridge and got to the first exhibit. In the darkness and shadow, the mannequins looked almost alive. I felt as though they might indeed be alive, and were only waiting for something to set them off, to start them moving.

I stared up into the massive tree of the first exhibit, the one with the men trying to get to their mistresses. In the darkness, they seemed like pitiful, sad figures, tragic.

I moved on, aimless, wanting to make the circuit of the entire Garden. I stopped at the crocodile enclosure, stood next to the railing on the concrete platform, listened to the birds chirping in the trees, and wondered again how Sister Moi had died. Had she been pushed? Had she been knocked unconscious and then thrown in? Or had she really committed suicide in this dreadful fashion? I could not bring myself to believe that—suicides don't just happen. Those who commit suicide always give plenty of signals well in advance. They don't just wake up one day and decide to let themselves be eaten by crocodiles. There's often a long history of mental suffering and anguish involved, leading to a sometimes inevitable conclusion. Sister Moi, from all appearances, did not have this history.

I sensed, more than heard, the approach of someone or other through the trees behind me. I turned in time to see three young men emerge along the path, dressed all in black and with less-than-kind looks on their faces.

Oh no.

They did not speak. They did not need to. I knew what they were going to do, knew there wasn't anything I could do to prevent it. In a rather business-like fashion, these mafia thugs took hold of me and began to administer what I hoped would be only a beating.

I was too old to roll with the punches, could do little more than feebly protest and try to keep my breath as they punched and kicked at me. Pain exploded in my body—in my shoulders, my stomach, my left leg, the back of my head, my face, my nose—surely they had broken it. I found myself on my knees, trying to curl up into a ball to protect myself. They were having none of it. They pulled at my arms, leaving my body free to receive more kicks and punches.

After a couple of minutes, they paused long enough to lift me up to my feet. Then they picked me up and tossed me over the fence into the crocodile enclosure.

I landed with a loud, awkward splash inside the concrete "river" below, completely flustered. I was so surprised I could do little more than sit there, my body screaming in protest, my mind quite dazed. It took awhile for the fact to dawn on me: they had thrown me into the croc enclosure. There was now nothing between me and the crocs but three orange sheets and a pair of flip-flops.

I scrambled to my feet in a panic.

The concrete wall that separated the enclosure from the Garden was about eight feet high—I could hardly reach the top of it. The fence itself was another five feet or so higher, and I did not see any way it could be reached and scaled.

I looked around. In the dim light, I saw crocodiles starting to stir, perhaps sensing that an early evening snack had been tossed into their midst.

What to do?

I was paralyzed with fear. I was a Buddhist monk, not a police officer—an old man who had gone to seed. I had no way to protect myself.

I jumped up, trying to reach the top of the concrete wall. Even if I could reach it, there was no telling whether I would have the strength to be able to hoist myself upwards enough to grab hold of the chain link fence. I jumped again. My fingers hit the concrete painfully, slid away. I fell back down into the water. A crocodile darted across a sandy area and slid silently into the river, heading in my direction. Damn! I jumped again. No luck. It was just an inch or two too high.

My heart raced in my chest. What was I going to do? I shouted, hoping someone could hear me. I saw a crocodile gliding through the water in my direction and started running—or at least moving as fast as I could with wet sheets hanging from my body while I splashed about in water that was thigh deep.

In the water, I would be no match for a crocodile, so I waded hurriedly to one of the sandy alcoves.

Crocodiles stirred, regarded me in the moonlight with their flat, emotionless eyes. I ran through their midst, trying to find a spot that was clear of them, but there were so many. Everywhere I looked, crocodile eyes looked back at me.

My hands shook and I could hardly breathe. What in the world was I supposed to do? Was I to become the next victim of Wat Yai and its dark secrets? Was I going to be stranded inside this enclosure with no way of escape?

A large crocodile sighted me, moved its bulk, began to head in my direction. I looked around, frantic for some way of escape, some way to defend myself. There were trees in the enclosure, but they were small, not the sort I could climb to get out of the crocodiles' path. I raced through the trees, bare-footed, my robes slipping off my body.

In the back of the enclosure I saw square concrete structures. They were only about chest height. They had openings in front, and some part of my brain suggested that they were places where female crocs could lay their eggs in privacy. I ran as quickly as I could toward these concrete structures, but out of the corner of my eye I saw an especially large crocodile headed in my direction. I did not need to be told that I didn't have enough time to get safely past him.

Adrenalin surged through my body.

I swerved. The crocodile snapped with its massive jaws. I felt pain in my right leg. I rushed past while the croc opened its jaws for another try. With a bound and full of giddy terror, I jumped up on the first concrete nesting site that I came to, ignoring the scraping of my skin against the concrete. I yanked my legs up, backed away.

The crocodiles started to gather around the nesting site, glaring up at me as if angry to have been denied their snack.

I looked at my right leg, saw the back of it covered in blood— the crocodile had either bitten me or had taken a good swipe at me with its deadly claws. I was in such a state that I did not even feel any pain, only bewilderment and confusion.

I screamed for help.

EIGHT

"Father Ananda?"

The light of a torch cut through the darkness, shining itself in my eyes. I raised a hand to my eyes to cut the glare.

"Father Ananda?"

It was Brother Pabhassaro.

"I need help," I said.

"What are you doing in the enclosure?"

"I was thrown in here!"

"You were thrown?"

"I need help, dammit!"

"Just stay where you are. Let me go turn the lights on."

His torchlight disappeared and I heard footsteps on what sounded like a concrete walkway. Soon enough lights came on, illuminating the enclosure, showing that a mere ten to fifteen feet separated me from freedom. Behind the nesting structures was more sandy ground and then a set of concrete stairs that led up to a chainlink gate and fence. All I had to do was get from where I was, across the sandy patch, and up the stairs.

My leg was bleeding profusely, though, and the pain of it suddenly began to impress itself on my awareness. I had lost two of my robes in the struggle, was now wearing the inner sarong-type garment around my waist. I tried to rip it, to get something to use as a tourniquet, but I was not strong enough and my hands wouldn't stop shaking.

Pabhassaro returned. I could see him clearly now, outlined in the lights. He was standing on a concrete walkway that ran behind the enclosure.

"Can you make a run for it?" he asked.

I looked at the distance, looked at my leg, had my doubts. My heart was beating wildly in my chest, and my whole body felt weak and exhausted. I wiped sweat from my face. "I got bitten," I called. "Or something. I need a tourniquet."

"Just stay there, then," he replied. He produced a ring full of keys, found the right one, opened the padlock that secured the chain wrapped around the gate to the enclosure. He hurried down the steps and ran over to where I was, seemingly unconcerned about the crocs. In a moment he was beside me on top of the nesting structure, looking at my leg in the glare of his torch.

"You didn't get bitten, just scratched," he said.

"Well, that's comforting," I said. "It still hurts."

He produced a box cutter, cut off a swatch of material from my robe, tied the tourniquet tightly around my calf. I grimaced. Pain raced up my leg and into my belly. The back of my head throbbed.

"Can you walk?" he asked.

I didn't know. I took his hand, tried to stand. I put weight on my injured leg. If I had to walk, I could. Running was another thing. Jumping down to the ground might prove impossible.

"Hold on a bit," Pabhassaro said. "I'll be back in a minute or two."

Without explanation, he jumped down to the sandy ground and hurried to the stairs and up to the gate, disappearing from view.

To say that I was completely flustered would be an understatement. I never would have expected mafia types to attack me inside a temple complex. Or to attack me at all, for that matter—we are, from birth, groomed to respect and revere monks. Not beat them up. Breaching that taboo would never have occurred to me. But our younger people had different ideas these days, and every time I turned around, I was being painfully reminded of that little fact of life. What was once sacred was now fair game.

I fought to get my breathing under control, to calm my nerves, to calm down. If the intent of my attackers had been to frighten me, they had done a good job. An excellent job, in fact.

Pabhassaro returned with what looked like an electric cattle prod, an instrument used to deliver electric shocks. While he stood guard below, zapping crocodiles that got too lose or too curious, I eased myself down from the nesting structure and hobbled over to the stairs, getting up them as fast as I could, and through the gate to safety.

NINE

"Do you always play with crocodiles?"

The nurse in the clinic's emergency room gave me a small smile as she asked this question.

"Only on Tuesdays," I replied. I struggled not to grimace and whine as the doctor poked and prodded at my wounds while the nurse assisted him.

Another wave of pain shot up my leg. The doctor was squeezing the blood from my wounds, he had said, to reduce the chance of infection. But every squeeze was making me feel faint and distinctly unwell. I had already sat through the painful process of dealing with a broken nose.

Another squeeze on my calf, another shot of pain.

I gritted my teeth.

"Pho, why didn't you tell me where you were going?" Jak asked. He was standing somewhere behind me—I could not see him.

I didn't answer the question. There was no answer to give. I had been a bit foolish to be wandering around on my own; I was now paying the price. What else could be said?

"Pho, I want to go home," Jak added. "Can we go home right now?"

"Not just yet," I said.

Another squeeze. Stars appeared before my eyes. I gripped the railing of the hospital bed tightly.

"Relax," the doctor said, "we're almost through."

Relax? Not on your life. And we hadn't even gotten to the stitches part. If this man didn't stop squeezing my wounds, I was going to start screaming.

"Pho, really," Jak said, his voice full of deadly earnest. "Let's go back to Wat Mahanat. I don't want to stay here anymore."

"We'll see," I said.

"You always say that when you don't want to give me a straight answer. I want to go home!"

"Be quiet!"

"No, I'm not going to be quiet! I want to leave this place!"

The nurse intervened before Jak's clock got completely wound up, telling him to either quiet down or go sit outside in the waiting room.

Silence descended. Angry, stony silence—I didn't need to see Jak's face to know that he was mad. It was like an electric current filling the room.

Just then there was a commotion outside the door and Jenjira and her troupe presented themselves. A camera started flashing before so much as a word of greeting had been uttered. I could not imagine what I must look like lying there on the stretcher while the doctor continued to torment me.

"Father Ananda!" Jenjira exclaimed, coming into my line of vision. "What on earth is going on?"

"I'll explain later," I said.

"Are you all right?"

"I'm fine," I said.

"You don't look fine. Who did this to you?"

"Anonymous thugs," I replied.

The nurse intervened again, asking Jenjira and her companions to wait outside. Jenjira promised she would, and there was peace and quiet once more as they all left.

"You sure do have a lot of friends," the nurse said, offering a small smile. Whether she was just pointing out a fact or making a comment on how annoying to her my friends were, I could not tell.

Another squeeze. Damn this doctor! Bloody stop already.

"Now let's sew this up," the doctor said cheerfully. "You're going to need about twelve stitches, Father Ananda. We'll be done in a jiffy."

I said nothing. The stitching part was much less painful than the prodding and poking and squeezing, and for that I was grateful. When they were done, they wrapped my calf in gauze and plenty of tape and I was free to carry on with my business. They wanted me to spend the night, "just for observation," but I detested hospitals and could not wait to leave.

"This is going to make a hell of a story," Jenjira said out in the waiting room, her face beaming with excitement.

"You don't have to run anything on me," I said.

"Oh yes we do—our readers will eat it up. *Famous monk attacked by thugs and thrown into crocodile enclosure at the Garden of Hell*—we can't lose."

"What did you find out about the kids at Wat Yai?"

"Something's fishy," she said right away. "The abbot was quite defensive when I talked to him, insisting everything was on the up and up."

"I hope you didn't believe him."

"Of course not. I asked him if I could be present when the next 'batch' comes in and he refused. I asked him if we could film the children and he refused. He knows the shit is about to hit the fan."

Jenjira was a short, heavyset woman who wore men's clothing and a man's haircut. She was prone to cursing, among other things. She was also very good at her job. One of her team members had a laptop computer on his lap, was "uploading" digital pictures of me in my agony. They could apparently, or so Jenjira explained, "upload" these pictures to the *Thai Rath* offices so that the story could be in tomorrow's newspaper. Wasn't technology wonderful?

"Please don't run anything on me," I said, my voice filled with pleading. "I've had enough publicity to last me a lifetime."

"Sorry, Father. No can do. A story's a story."

"I'd really appreciate it if you didn't."

"Sorry. And anyway, I think you'll find people will be more sympathetic with your cause if I run a picture of you and your broken nose."

I tried to imagine what I must look like with my bandages and taped-up nose and bald head and decided it wouldn't be all that pretty.

"We're going to go find a hotel or something," she said. "Call me if anything else happens, okay? Otherwise I'll see you tomorrow."

I promised I would call if anything else happened—not that I was going to be up for much of anything else except a good rest—and off she went.

Jak now took my arm and gazed at me with a mix of pity and anger in his eyes.

"We're not going back there," he said, more a question than a statement.

"We've got nowhere else to stay," I pointed out.

Kusalo cleared his throat, reminding me that he was waiting to drive us back to Wat Yai in the temple van.

"Let's go," I said.

"Sure. And get yourself killed," Jak said, his voice dripping with sarcasm. "That'll be fun."

"Nothing's going to happen," I said.

"Yeah, right. Like I believe you."

"Just trust me, okay?"

He said nothing. His lips tightened into a tense line and he would not look at me.

CHAPTER SIX

"A slower walking pace reveals songbirds never seen before."
—*The Sage's Tao Te Ching: A New Interpretation, #62*

ONE

I felt lousy the next morning. One would, I suppose, after a beating and a crocodile scare and a broken nose. I told myself I should be grateful that I hadn't been killed, but gratitude was hard to come by. I could hardly sit up and see straight, much less count my blessings.

Jak had already gotten up, had done his morning business and put on his robes. He was sitting by the side of my mat, watching me with unreadable eyes.

"Well," I said, sensing that he was still in a mood. Thanks to the bandages on my nose, my voice sounded nasal, funny.

"You're not going anywhere," he said.

"Not even to the bathroom?" *Nod even to dah bafwomb?*

"Not even to the bathroom. If you so much as get off that mat, I'll break your arm. And all the rest of your bones, for that matter."

Obviously he was in a very wintry mood.

"I'm so mad at you," he exclaimed forcefully. His eyes began to tear up. "How could you be so stupid, going to the Garden at night by yourself?"

I felt sheepish.

"You want to get yourself killed?" he added, warming up to his subject. "Is that it? You don't care about anybody else, just yourself? You don't care about how anybody else feels? You don't care about how I feel? What's going to happen to me if something happens to you? Don't you care about that?"

I said nothing.

"I'm so mad at you," he exclaimed again, "I don't know what to do with myself." There were real tears in his eyes now and he wiped at them angrily. He refused to look at me, embarrassed by this unmonkly show of emotion.

Novice Jak was fiercely attached to me and I was fiercely attached to him. I understood his feelings. He was afraid of losing me. He'd suffered a right and proper scare and now he needed to let off some steam. He wasn't really angry—he was just scared.

"Everything's going to be fine," I said. I didn't know what else to say, how to make the situation better.

"You're not going anywhere today unless I go with you," he said crossly. "And if you have any sense, you'll buy us two bus tickets so we can go home and get away from this crazy place."

"We can't leave just yet," I said.

"Pho!"

"Jak, think for a minute: What about those children? We have to help them. We can't just run off and leave them behind."

The look on his face said he didn't much care one way or the other, but he held his tongue.

"Anyway," I added, "if they wanted to kill me, they would have done so last night. They were just trying to give us a good scare."

"They certainly succeeded, although I'd be surprised if anything got through that fat head of yours. Next time you might not be so lucky. You ever stop to think about that?"

"There's not going to be a next time."

"Yeah, right. Like I believe you. And how do you know they didn't intend to kill you? Maybe they thought the crocodiles would finish you off."

"Unlikely."

"Like they finished off that nun."

Sister Moi.

I gave Jak a long look. He had triggered something in my mind. Why hadn't Sister Moi been able to get out of the enclosure, as I had? I thought I knew the answer, but wasn't sure. Chances were pretty good that Sister Moi had already been dead by the time she'd been thrown into the enclosure—dead or otherwise incapacitated.

"It'll be fine," I said.

Of course both of us knew that was probably a lie.

TWO

"What were you thinking?" Abbot Uddi demanded. He looked so furious that I expected him to start spitting nine-inch nails at any moment. "How could you sic that reporter on me like that? How can you accuse me of being involved in child trafficking? Would you look at this newspaper?"

He tossed the newspaper at me. The latest issue of *Thai Rath* fell apart as it fell to the floor at my feet. The hard lines on the abbot's face were even harder than usual.

"If there's nothing to hide, there's nothing to worry about," I said, trying to sound as nonchalant as I could. It had, after all, been a long time since I'd received a dressing down by an abbot. I had all but forgotten what it was like.

"You could have talked to me first," he said. "You didn't have to go to the press."

"I could say the same," I replied.

"What's that supposed to mean?"

"Who set the mafia guys on me? You?"

"Me? What else are you accusing me of?"

"I'm not accusing you of anything, but I was attacked, in your Garden, in your temple complex, by a group of thugs. Doesn't that bother you?"

"Frankly, no. I've got more important things to worry about."

"Like a trafficking ring?"

His eyes narrowed down to slits.

"How do you explain the license?" I asked.

"I don't have to answer your questions. And I want you out of my monastery. I don't care who sent you."

"I'm afraid I can't do that," I said.

"Why not?"

"Because there's a murderer running around this monastery and I am going to catch him. Not to mention the fact that I don't answer to you and you have no right to interfere in my investigation. You have no right to be telling me what I can and cannot do."

"We'll see what sort of rights you have," he vowed, turning on his heel and stalking off.

In the silence after his departure, both Kusalo and Jak stared at me, troubled looks on their faces.

"That went reasonably well," I said.

They did not seem to concur. In fact, they were speechless.

THREE

It did not take long for the parking lot at Wat Yai to fill up with media vehicles of all shapes and sizes. Now that *Thai Rath* had broken the news, all the other media outlets showed up to make sure they got their fare share of the pickings. And the pickings were certainly scrumptious.

As the monks returned from their alms rounds that morning, they were accosted by microphones and flashing cameras and video technicians and more questions than they knew what to do with.

I stayed inside the dorm building, afraid to show my bandaged face. *Thai Rath* already had a mugshot of me on its front page, with a huge headline: *Monk attacked by thugs at Wat Yai*. That was enough. I didn't want every other newspaper in the country to have the same thing on its front page tomorrow.

"It's madness out there," Kusalo said.

"You're going to have to go talk to them," I said. "Isn't that your job?" He was, after all, the "face" of the monastery.

"But tell them what, Father Ananda? I don't know anything more than you do."

"You can just say the matter is being investigated and you'll get back to them when you have concrete news. That'll hold them off."

He did not seem convinced, made no effort to go outside.

I couldn't blame him.

If we wanted breakfast, though, we were going to have to brave the storm. We were going to have to do something. Eventually we decided that Novice Jak could nip over to the breakfast hall and collect some food for the three of us. With a frown, Jak went to the door and on outside as Kusalo and I settled down to wait for his return.

"Aren't you worried about what the abbot said?" Kusalo asked.

"Why should I be?" I replied.

"Well, he is the abbot."

"True enough, but I don't answer to him. I answer to the Maha Thera Samakhom—they wanted an investigation, and now they're getting one. Anyway, if the abbot doesn't have anything to hide, what's the worry? We'll get things sorted out and that will be that. No harm done."

"What if he does have something to hide?"

"Let the chips fall where they will."

He pursed his lips together, did not seem comforted by my cavalier attitude.

"Abbots can be replaced," I said, trying to offer some encouragement. "It won't be the end of the world. And he won't be the first abbot run out of office. And he won't be the first abbot caught dabbling in unholy business. They're a dime a dozen, if the newspapers are anything to go by."

"I suppose you're right," he said, but carefully not looking at me.

We lapsed into silence.

I was hungry and it seemed that Jak was taking forever to bring us something to eat. Had he stopped to eat first? It wouldn't surprise me. Yet I thought we had made it clear that the three of us would eat together as soon as he returned. After many more minutes had gone by, I said, "I wonder where that kid is."

"Your novice?"

"With our food, yes. What's taking Jak so long?"

He offered a frown of worry. "Want me to go check?"

I did, if only for my own selfish reasons. I was hungry, after all, not to mention thirsty and out of sorts. I wanted to eat breakfast and get on with the day—I had a lot to do.

Kusalo left the dorm room. Silence fell. I thought—absently—about Pol Maj Gen Chao and his men. Were the threats in his "love letters" real, or was he just blowing off steam, stewing in his own juices? Would he really kill me if he had the chance? Was it safe to remain at Wat Mahanat, or would I be well advised to move on? Was Jak in any danger? But surely they wouldn't involve a novice in the dispute. I was the one who had made Chao lose face, not Jak.

It occurred to me then that I did not want to leave Wat Mahanat. All my friends were there. Kittisaro, the abbot's secretary; Tammarato, my mentor; Udena, the maintenance man; so many others. I could not picture myself living anywhere else, had no desire to move on, no desire to experience new things. I was old and set in my ways and preferred to keep things just as they were.

Yet I had no doubts about Chao and his abilities. If he wanted to do me harm, he would certainly succeed. And I gathered that his reasons for writing the love letters were to unnerve me, to let me experience doubt and hesitation about my future, to run me off like a dog with its tail between its legs. That would make him happy, wouldn't it? The supposedly great Father Ananda having to hightail it to the countryside because he had stepped on the wrong person's toes.

We Thais can be an unforgiving lot, that was certainly true. We held our grudges close to the vest, nursing them, fanning the flames, ready at a moment's notice to get revenge and satisfaction. Revenge is a dish best served up cold, or so the saying goes. Chao was not likely to forget what I had done, and was not likely to ever forgive and "move on." On the contrary. In fact, I would be surprised if he didn't try to avenge himself in one way or another. That would be the Thai way of doing things. It was only a matter of time now, wasn't it?

It took Kusalo about five minutes to return. When he did, he returned alone.

"I couldn't find him," he said, throwing a worried glance in my direction.

"You what?"

"I couldn't find him," he repeated.

"What do you mean, you couldn't find him?"

"He's gone."

"Gone?"

"Yes. He's gone. I checked the bathrooms, everywhere. I asked around—no one saw him over in the breakfast hall. He's just ... gone."

"Gone?" I stood up, wobbled a bit, ignored my aches and pains. "How can he just be gone?" It was a stupid question and I knew it. But I couldn't stop myself from asking.

"I don't know Father Ananda. He's just gone. Unless he's hiding in one of the *kuti* or something, and I can't imagine why he would be doing that. Otherwise I didn't see hide nor hair of him and I looked everywhere."

I searched Kusalo's face. Was he telling the truth? Obviously he was. Why would he lie? And yet—how could Jak just be "gone"? People don't just disappear into thin air. I was having a great deal of trouble wrapping my mind around this thought, mostly because I didn't want to. Its implications were too frightening, too overwhelming.

"There must be some mistake," I said. It had to be a mistake, an oversight, something perfectly simple and easily explained away. It had to be. "Go check again."

"Okay, I will, but I'm telling you, he's gone."

He left without saying anything further and I watched him from the window of the dorm, puzzled, an uneasy feeling in the pit of my stomach.

If Jak had indeed "disappeared"—well, my mind didn't want to pursue that thought. Suddenly I was thinking of mafia thugs, an angry abbot who had just made some veiled threats against me, a child trafficking ring and a thirteen-year-old novice with a crippled leg who could so easily get caught up in the middle of it all, perhaps used as a bargaining chip—or worse.

Surely they wouldn't harm an innocent child? But who was I kidding—these were people operating a trafficking ring! What did the life of one more child mean? Less than nothing.

My gut tightened into a painful knot.

Had they taken Jak? If any harm came to that child, I would never be able to forgive myself. Never. Not in a million years. I was responsible for that boy's safety, his well-being. If he came to harm—even the thought of it made the breath freeze in my chest.

I stared out the window and when I saw Kusalo returning, sans our novice, a worm of fear began crawling around inside my belly.

FOUR

I hurried outside.

Kusalo caught sight of me, offered a grimace and a shrug. That was enough to explain that his second search had not been any more fruitful than the first. He adjusted his glasses nervously and his handsome face seemed a bit pale, a bit pinched.

The media also caught sight of me and began streaming in my direction, their cameras flashing, looks of crazed eagerness in their eyes. "Father Ananda!" "Is it true?" "Who did this to you?" "Is there really a trafficking ring, Father Ananda?" "Are you a representative of the Maha Thera Samakhom now?" "What do you know about the nun who killed herself?" "Father Ananda, what can you tell us about the dead monk?" "Are you in charge now?"

I ignored their hollered questions, took Kusalo by the arm, headed in the direction of the breakfast hall. The media folks followed, shouting questions all the way. Wasn't I the one who said I wanted to shake things loose? I had succeeded, hadn't I?

In the breakfast hall, the monks were dining, offered me puzzled looks as I raised my voice and asked about my novice monk. Had he been seen? Blank looks. Had anyone seen him at all? More blank looks. Could we organize a search party, do it immediately? There was a bit of grumbling but several monks left off breakfast and got up to offer assistance.

"Search the *kuti*," I suggested. "And the Garden. And wherever else you can think of. He's only been gone for ten, twenty minutes. He can't have gone far."

"But what do you think happened to him?" one of the monks asked.

For that, I had no answer, least none that I cared to give with reporters standing around and cameras flashing.

When the media realized they weren't going to get a rise out of me, they gave up, went back to the parking lot, scribbling in notebooks, checking over equipment, talking on cell phones, pecking away at laptops. With the volunteer monks, I helped search for Jak, but the search turned up nothing.

How could a novice monk simply disappear into thin air without anyone having seen anything?

I led Kusalo back to the dorm building, stood on its steps, looked around. If Jak had gone after food, as we had requested, he would have to walk down the path between two large buildings—the main *sala* and one of the funeral halls—to get to the breakfast hall. Or at least that would have been the shortest, quickest route. I tried to retrace his footsteps. We went down the path between the buildings. At the end, as we turned a corner, the breakfast hall was almost within sight, but not really, thanks to the abbot's office and various trees and parked vehicles. Had Jak been standing right in this spot, he could have been nabbed, hustled into a vehicle and driven off, with no one the wiser.

I continued on, heading to the breakfast hall. No other spot offered such an advantage as that first spot had—they were out in the open and Jak would have been easily seen.

"Someone must have kidnapped him," I said to Kusalo.

"What on earth for?"

"Are you as naive as you appear to be?"

"What's that supposed to mean?"

"They'd kidnap him if they wanted to have something to use for leverage."

"They?"

"Yes. *They. Them.* The mafia guys. The ones who beat me up. The one who beat me over the head the other night out in back by the rubbish. Your abbot, who just hollered at me."

"They can't just kidnap someone in broad daylight," Kusalo pointed out.

I said nothing. The man was either much denser than he appeared to be or was enormously slow on the uptake.

I was surprised when I looked down and saw that my hands were shaking like leaves on a tree in the middle of a monsoon storm. I was afraid for Jak, of what they might do to him. I was afraid of never seeing him again, of being responsible for his death. I would never forgive myself if he came to harm, just as my own son had come to harm so many years ago now. The thought made me physically ill. There wasn't much of anything I wouldn't do for that boy and these people probably knew it.

"So what are we going to do?" Kusalo asked, clasping his hands together nervously.

That was a pertinent question. As for an answer, I had no idea.

FIVE

A nun came hurrying toward us.

"Father Ananda!"

What did she want? What else was going wrong?

"Father Ananda, they took the children!" the nun exclaimed.

"What children?"

The nun paused to catch her breath. "The abbot ordered all the children to be sent away—the lorry just left."

She turned, heading back the way she had come. We followed, through the monastery complex, out into the back, through the gate in the concrete wall, down to the buildings where the children had been housed.

Out of the corner of my eye, I saw reporters trailing after us, figured that was a good thing. When we got there, we found that some reporters were already there—they were taking pictures and talking to the nuns.

"What's going on?" I demanded when I caught sight of Sister Mettha.

"They're gone now," she said, a twinge of bitterness in her voice. "The abbot said we were closing the program down, that the children were to be sent back to Bangkok right away. The lorry just left."

Off in the distance I could see a lorry driving on a dirt road, kicking up a dust storm.

"Why didn't you come and get me?" I demanded.

"I tried. You weren't at breakfast with the others—I had no idea where you were."

Without the presence of the children, the imposing concrete buildings seemed lifeless, desolate, all the more oppressive.

"Did you get the license plate number of the lorry?"

Sister Mettha shook her head.

"Did anyone?" I asked, somewhat exasperated.

"There was no time," she said. "The abbot was rushing us to get the kids dressed and ready to go."

"Why the rush?"

"I don't know. We only do what we're told, Father Ananda. We don't ask questions."

"Father Ananda, what's wrong?" a reporter asked.

I looked at him. He was one of the more mangy reporter types—long hair, casual dress, almost a deliberate disregard for personal hygiene. He was Chinese, obviously—he had several long hairs hanging from a mole to the right of his lips. What to tell him? Yet a thought occurred to me.

A gaggle of reporters stood in the driveway, chatting, comparing notes, working with their equipment. I approached, asked if anyone had taken pictures of the lorry. No one had. But fortunately one of the television outlets had taken footage of the lorry as it had left.

"Can I see it?" I asked.

"If you want," the technician said. He seemed pleased to be asked. I waited patiently as he fiddled with his dials and knobs and buttons. Eventually the picture of a lorry came into focus. It was very tightly covered with a tarpaulin and no children could be seen—they must have all been packed inside and hidden away from view. But the license plate on the back was in plain sight.

"Can you stop it there?" I asked.

He did.

I jotted down the license plate number and thanked him. I even asked the poor fellow for his cell phone so that I could make a call to Bangkok. I called Kittisaro, gave him the license plate number, and asked him to notify Lt Somchai at the Silom Station, my good friend and co-conspirator.

"Ask him to run the plates, put out a notice on the wire—we've got to find that truck and those children. Tell him to do it as soon as possible."

"Not a problem," Kittisaro said.

"And one other thing," I said.

"What?"

"Jak is missing."

SIX

In the midst of this ruckus, life at Wat Yai went on. Tourists still arrived in their busloads, tickets were sold, tours of the Garden of Hell were given, but now by a new monk who seemed far less sure of himself than his recently deceased predecessor. Monks—mostly juniors and novices—swept the grounds. Dogs lounged about, chased after chickens, snoozed in quiet, shady places. If one didn't know any better, one would assume it was just a normal day at a normal country temple out in the boondocks.

Kusalo had gathered six fellow monks and we were conducting a sweep of the Garden of Hell, looking—again—for any trace of Jak. We poked behind trees, in the heavy brush between the main exhibits. We searched the crocodile enclosure. We beat the bushes. But Jak was nowhere to be seen.

The sun overhead was hot on my bare head and as the morning wore on, I felt increasing unwell. The beating had taken more out of me than I cared to admit. I was not a young pup anymore, no longer able to bounce back from such unexpected unpleasantness. My body wanted rest, time to mend. My chest hurt—large bruises were testament to the kicks I had received. My nose throbbed. I had to breathe through my mouth.

Yet, there was going to be no rest for me, not until I had discovered the whereabouts of my novice monk. Partly because I'm somewhat of a perfectionist, I always had to double-check the work of others. I simply couldn't bring myself to trust that they had done a good job. It was a trait that I was embarrassed by, but I couldn't help it. So now, beating the bushes and looking for Jak, I made another circuit of the Garden on my own, this time checking out the places where others had already looked, hoping to find something they had missed.

There were more exhibits than I had at first thought, many of them small, tucked away in corners here and there—a bear mauling a scantily clad woman, a snake eating a man, a demon attacking a young girl. They had been designed to be part of the landscaping, as it were. Each of these small displays had a concrete base on which the display sat. I checked them over carefully. I checked behind them. I pushed my way through heavy brush, walked long-disused paths, searched through dense groves of trees. I came across a display missing its victim—the one Moi had messed with, most likely.

Jak, where are you?

Jak was like a son to me. I had grown far too attached, far too concerned with his well being. It wasn't good for a monk to be so attached, so easily disturbed. Unlike the Lord Buddha, I was not yet perfect. I couldn't bring myself to be indifferent to the suffering of others. I couldn't maintain my peace of mind while those I loved and cared for were in trouble. Just couldn't do it. Wanted to, but could not.

Despite my best efforts, the search turned up precisely nothing. I talked to Brother Pabhassaro, enlisted his help, but not even his detailed knowledge of the Garden and its exhibits wasn't of any use.

Jak was simply not to be found.

Since all else had failed, I went to the media congregating in the parking lot and started giving interviews.

SEVEN

Jak did not show up and as the day wore on, my nerves grew increasingly worse. I was a Buddhist monk; I was supposed to be calm, collected, detached, serene, with eyes that smiled and lips that were playful. I was anything but. I was distracted, anxious, annoyed, frustrated, fearful—I would be pulling hair out but for the fact that I didn't have any.

Why had I brought Jak in the first place? Why hadn't I given more thought to his safety? More importantly, what had become of my novice? And would he come to harm? The thought caused my insides to squeeze up painfully.

I thought I knew who the killer was, but thus far I had precious little evidence. Only a theory. An idea. Of all the people that I had talked to and interviewed and considered, only one name remained on my list. Only one name made sense. In fact, the person I was thinking about was perfectly obvious.

But how to prove it?

It was late in the afternoon. The monks had gathered in the main *sala* for the funeral chants for Brother Pandito. I was alone in the dorm room, flat on my back, a hand across my brow, lost in thought. My body might be failing me, but my mind wasn't. In fact, my mind was in overdrive, jumping from one thought to the next, trying to stitch all the pieces of this garment together.

When my cell phone rang, I grabbed it, discovered that Kittisaro in Bangkok was on the other end.

"We've identified the owner of the truck," he said right off.

"And who is it?"

"A certain Mr. A. You know who I'm talking about?"

Indeed I did.

"Has the truck itself been located?"

"Thanks to you, the whole country is looking for it—you look good on the television, you know, what with that bandage on your face. You sounded a bit funny, though."

"Thanks."

"We had a good laugh."

"Yeah, it's hilarious. Did they find the truck yet?"

"Not yet. We just have to wait and see what develops."

Kittisaro rang off after promising to keep me updated.

At that moment, the door to the dorm opened and a familiar figure stepped inside, followed by four of his cronies:

Pol Maj Gen Chao. Sender of my love letters.

Oh damn.

What else could go wrong?

I struggled to sit up, to prepare myself for what would likely be another beating—or worse.

"The famous Father Ananda," Chao said grandly, indicating me with a wave of his arm. "So nice to see you again."

"What do you want?" I asked, trying not to sound as afraid as I felt.

"Oh," he said, then sighed. "I want so many things. You wouldn't understand. A man of the world has, shall we say, certain appetites—certain desires. Sometimes those desires come into conflict."

I rose unsteadily to my feet. "Is that right?"

"Indeed it is, Father Ananda. Right now I'm feeling most conflicted. The urge to kill you remains strong, yet I find that you might be useful."

"Useful?"

"The enemy of my enemy is my friend," Chao said cryptically.

I struggled to maintain my composure. What did the man want? If he was going to beat me or kill me, why not just get it over with? Why the chitchat?

"I'm afraid I don't follow," I said, when he remained silent, peering at me with intent, bright eyes.

"Of course you don't," Chao said. "I'm here to help, Father Ananda. I can assure you that no harm will come to you, despite my recent letters. You see, you've suddenly become somewhat of an asset."

"And how is that?"

"You're the enemy of my enemy. It may be that in exchange for making me loose face, you can now do something of benefit to me. It's a complicated bit of calculus but I think you might be able to manage it."

"Manage what?"

"Catching your bad guy, obviously."

"You're going to help me do that?"

"What are friends for?"

"I didn't know we were friends."

"We are now. Have you found your novice yet?"

I admitted that I had not. "Were you the one who snatched him?"

"Goodness no!" He laughed as if the question was amusing. "I haven't got a clue as to where he is. Anyway, I didn't come here to talk to you about your novice. I came to talk about the abbot and his brother Mr. A. You see, the people I work for consider Mr. A to be very annoying. They'd like nothing more than a bit of press exposure of his misdeeds, which you seem to be generating rather easily. Mr. A has gotten too powerful for his own good, or so my sources tell me. So the more you humble him, the happier we'll be."

"Isn't that nice," I said. I was trying to shut down a human trafficking ring; he was trying to jump into the party and make his own position stronger.

"What if I said I knew where a certain lorry was, at this very moment in time? Would that be of interest to you?"

"Depends on what it will cost me," I said.

"Just a little chitchat with the media. That's all. You can trust me on that. I've even brought along some photos that you might find highly interesting."

One of the members of his entourage stepped forward with a file folder, which Chao took and handed to me.

I flipped the folder open, discovered pictures of Mr. A in a poppy field, overseeing workers. Poppies, of course, were harvested to produce heroin. And Mr. A, of course, had famously denied having anything at all to do with poppies or heroin or any drugs. In other words, the pictures would make Mr. A look like the liar that he was.

"All you need do," Chao said, "is hand these photos over to that enterprising journalist friend of yours—what's her name? That *tom*."

"Jenjira."

"Yes. Jenjira. Let her do an expose—and let the media feasting begin!"

"Why don't you just give them to her yourself?"

"That's part of the deal, Father Ananda. No one is to know where these photos came from. That's the catch. I have my reasons and I'll say no more about it. Are you game?"

In other words, did I want to do his dirty work for him, in exchange for information as to where the lorry was, information that might lead to the rescuing of those children?

"There's got to be more to it than that," I said.

"Oh, there is," Chao readily agreed. "You don't think making Mr. A lose face like this is going to come cheap, do you? I can assure you it won't. You'll be high on his shit list, if not at the very top."

I glanced at the folder in his hands, bit at my lip. It was a devil's bargain. It was bad enough that I had upset Chao and his minions; now he wanted me to upset an honest-to-gosh godfather, with no way of knowing the sort of consequences that would bring. Yet what choice was there? If I wanted to help those children—and I did, especially the little Cambodian girl La-or—then I would have to comply.

"I'll make a deal," I said. "You tell me where the truck is and when the police have found it and rescued those children, I'll have a chat with the media on your behalf. And no more love letters."

"And you'll keep quiet about our conversation too, won't you," he replied, "because if you don't, your own reputation will be smeared. Imagine: the famous Father Ananda tarnishing the reputation of an outstanding citizen just to get something he wanted. How will your fans react to that?"

"No one need know," I said.

"That's what I like about you, Father Ananda. You're so predictable. So concerned about the riffraff that you'll do anything to help them. You must be wracking up a great deal of merit."

I said nothing. He handed me a piece of paper with an address on it—the location of the lorry.

"One more thing," he said. "I take it you've been to visit the Garden. Let me just say that not everything over there is what it appears to be. I'll say no more—let you figure it out for yourself."

Before turning on his heel and departing, he offered a *wai* gesture of respect, but made certain to keep his folded hands low so as to show a certain bit of disrespect. I offered a similar ambiguous *wai* and that was the end of that.

Trembling, I lay back on the mat and took a deep breath.

EIGHT

I called Kittisaro and gave him the address that Chao had supplied.

"You got this from Chao?" he asked, incredulous.

I tried to explain the situation as best I could and as quickly as I could, since I wanted Kittisaro to call the police and alert them as soon as possible.

After he rang off, I gathered my nerves, ignored the throbbing in my face—my nose was hurting terribly—and left the dorm. It was just past six in the evening and the funeral chants for Brother Pandito had just gotten underway. I walked in the direction of the funeral hall, scanned the faces of the monks gathered, saw the monk I expected to see there, hurriedly turned away. I would have about twenty minutes.

Out in the midst of the *kuti*, I found this monk's bungalow and hurried up the stairs. I was all nerves, afraid I would be caught, thus tipping off my prime suspect. I didn't want him to know that I was on to him, not just yet, not until I was ready to confront him.

A perusal of his things turned up more than I could have hoped for, particularly bank statements and letters from Brother Panya to Sister Moi—letters that left no doubt as to his guilt. He had indeed raped her, admitted as much in letters that were addressed to her. In the letters he begged her to consider leaving the monastery with him, getting married, and settling down to raise a family. "Our first child is on its way!" "You know I could never love anyone more than I love you!" "Please trust me—our life together will be smooth." "I'll get a job." "We'll live with my parents." "You know it has to be this way." "If not for my sake, do it for the sake of the baby."

I would have to verify that the handwriting was indeed that of Brother Panya, which I could do by looking at his file.

I was on my hands and knees, pawing through things but trying not to disturb them too much—I didn't want my search to be noticed. But it was hard. There was so much stuff piled into this *kuti*. I wasn't going to have enough time to search through it all. So I hurried, found a few pieces of evidence that would be incontrovertible—like my crumpled up letter with coffee stains on it and a robe in need of patching up—then left the *kuti* in haste.

I walked briskly through the trees. The sky was darkening, night was falling. The drone of the chanting went on. I made my way to the parking lot, searching for Jenjira.

"Don't ask me where I got these from," I said to her, turning over the evidence, explaining as best I could what I thought was going on at this monastery. I also gave her the file from Chao. She whistled in thinly repressed glee at the sight of the photos—there wasn't a doubt in the world that those photos wouldn't make it to the front pages tomorrow. I did not care about that. I cared about the children and shutting down the trafficking ring. I cared about La-or and Jak, my novice. Perhaps I was a fool but I cared about justice, fairness, the rule of law.

I left Jenjira and headed to the Garden of Hell, remembering Chao's words: *Let me just say that not everything over there is what it appears to be.*

I had no idea what he meant by that, but obviously he was trying to tell me something, to point out something that I had missed. What? I did not know. I was determined to find out.

The Garden was still open and some of the mourners roamed here and there, rather than sitting down with the others in the funeral hall to listen to the monks' chanting. Most of those roaming about in the Garden were younger people who no doubt thought that chanting was boring.

Let me just say that not everything over there is what it appears to be.

What was he referring to? I started at the beginning and examined each of the exhibits closely. What had I missed?

The exhibits were all as I remembered them, only now I was looking more carefully, wondering what secrets I might have missed. As I searched I thought of Jak and my belly ached with anxiety and not a little fear. If he had been snatched, what better place to hide him than right here in this Garden?

I searched the length and breadth of the crocodile enclosure, wanting to be absolutely sure that Jak wasn't in it. We had already searched it once—Pabhassaro had even checked the nesting enclosures at my behest—but I was feeling rather obsessive and worried. The last thing I wanted was to find Jak half-eaten by these idiotic show animals.

My search revealed nothing.

I continued the circuit, checking out the main exhibits. I ignored the looks I received from the Garden's visitors as I poked and prodded and tried to figure out what Chao had meant.

Let me just say that not everything over there is what it appears to be.

What was that supposed to mean?

CHAPTER SEVEN

*"Not trying to control life means freedom
to be guided by the Tao."*
—-The Sage's Tao Te Ching: A New Interpretation, #36

ONE

Officials from the Immigration Department arrived that evening at Wat Yai and began going through the books on Abbot Uddi's supposed repatriation program. Abbot Uddi himself was taken into custody, was to be held until it could be determined what, precisely, was going on with his repatriation program, and what sort of charges would be brought against him, if any. It was still not clear whether he was involved at all and he was not slow to protest his innocence.

The lorry was found exactly where Chao had said it would be found; the children were retrieved and taken into Immigration custody. All were accounted for, even little La-or.

That was all well and good, but my novice was still missing and a murderer was still walking free at Wat Yai and I had to figure out what to do to rectify both situations.

My head pounded. What I really wanted to do was sleep, rest, recover. I had been pushing myself too hard that day; my body was complaining, demanding rest, reminding me of the punishment it had recently endured.

But there was no time to rest.

I went to the Garden in search of Pabhassaro. After the skull bridge there is a small path that leads off to the left. Following that path led one to the entrance to Pabhassaro's maintenance area—the door was carefully positioned to be screened by trees and all but unnoticeable. I approached the door, found it open, let myself inside.

I was accosted by the tools of Pabhassaro's trade: wheel barrows to deliver food for the crocodiles; rolls of fencing, lengths of chain; three small exhibits in various stages of completion; a workshop with tools, numerous pieces of wood, foam, plaster molds, and Pabhassaro himself, sitting in the midst of this mess drinking what appeared to be fruit juice but what was probably alcohol.

"I need your help," I said.

"What makes you think I'm going to help you?"

"The same thing that makes me think that you're not the one murdering people around here. A feeling, I guess. Are you going to help me or not?"

He did not seem pleased by this imposition on his free time. The look on his face was one of annoyance. "So what is it you need?" he asked.

"I was told that this Garden is not all it appears to be."

"What does that mean?"

"I'm not sure. But I thought you would have a better idea than I would."

His face scrunched up in thought. "You must be referring to the tunnels."

"Tunnels?"

"Yes," he said. "Beneath the Garden. We store stuff down there. I could show you, if that would help."

Excited, I said that it would and he got to his feet and led me out into the Garden proper. He walked the circuit, then departed from the path to go stand in front of an exhibit of a bear mauling a young woman. He gave the bear's flank a push and the entire exhibit slid back to reveal a ladder going down into darkness.

"What's down there?" I asked, feeling a bit suspicious, a bit nervous.

"Why don't you go find out?" Pabhassaro replied.

If Pabhassaro was the killer, I was making a huge mistake by trusting him. I did not believe he was, but the possibility existed. He was number two on my list, after all, a suspect who worked in the Garden where the bodies of Sister Moi and Brother Pandito had been found, a suspect who had the physical strength to carry out the killings and their aftermath, a suspect who seemed moody and irritated—just the sort of person who might commit murder. And on top of all that, he wasn't exactly a friendly, helpful type.

It was clear that he wanted a demonstration that I trusted him. So, feeling uneasy but trying hard to disguise it, I put my foot on the first rung of the ladder and began to descend. If he locked me inside the tunnel, I had no idea how I would get out or what I could do to stop him.

I proceeded anyway. At the bottom of the ladder, I retrieved the torch from my monk's bag, flipped it on, looked around. I saw shelves, mostly, packed with all sorts of things—dried foodstuffs, cardboard boxes, more tools, bits of fencing, huge chains, stacks of lumber, buckets of paint, on and on.

I heard Pabhassaro descending, moved out of the way.

Was this the place that Chao had wanted me to discover? And if it was, what was I supposed to be seeing?

Pabhassaro flipped on an overhead light, showing me that the tunnel was reinforced with sturdy boards and had a concrete floor.

"It was built during World War II," he explained. "There was a lot of paranoia back in those days. Anyway, what you see is what you get. There's another room further down if you want to go have a look."

I did. I followed as Pabhassaro led the way between the tall rows of shelving. We passed Buddha images that were old and in disrepair. It wasn't proper to throw them away, so they were kept on shelves, left to age as the years went by. We passed by old spirit houses, which likewise could not be thrown away. We passed a variety of old mannequins in need of repair or replacement altogether. Another shelf contained several bags of concrete; another contained an enormous supply of small bricks.

The air was damp, close, musty smelling.

We passed by more shelves. I saw boxes of documents, ancient scrolls rolled up and stored in plastic bags, more Buddha images, old pieces of furniture—an ancient camera, several typewriters, an old turntable from the seventies, boxes of old books, junk and more junk.

Monasteries tended to collect junk because it's not proper to throw away items that have been donated—even if the monastery doesn't need them or want them. They have to be kept. Good monks try to give the items away to those who visit them; if one didn't, such items had a tendency to start piling up. I can't recall how many electric fans and umbrellas I had been given over the years. The number was certainly far higher than I could ever possibly use in this and twenty other lifetimes. So I gave them away every chance I got. Most monks did the same. But still the stuff kept collecting.

At the end of this passage was an old wooden door. Pabhassaro pushed the door open and motioned for me to enter and check it out. I did. Pabhassaro came in behind me and the next thing I knew I was flat on my face—he had pushed me from behind.

I rolled, turned over, tried to find his face in the darkness.

"The great Father Ananda," he said, chuckling. "We had no idea that you were so stupid."

I struggled to get my robes untangled, to get to my feet. I heard noise—Pabhassaro's footsteps—then the slamming of the door. Blind in the darkness, I walked cautiously forward trying to find the door. I did. It was locked.

Pabhassaro called from the other side. "Enjoy your stay, Mr. Hot Shot Monk from the Big City."

"Let me out of here!" I demanded.

"Sorry, Father. Nothing doing. Don't bother trying to escape. You'll discover that it's impossible."

"Let me out!" I shouted.

In response, I heard the sound of retreating footsteps.

Fuming, I banged on the door and yelled—not that it did any good.

TWO

It must have been an oversight on Pabhasarro's part: I still had my torch. I dug around in my bag, found it, turned it on.

I was in a small cellar and I was not alone: Jak was lying on the ground, hands tied behind his back, duct tape across his mouth.

"Jak?" I said. "Are you alright?"

As if to answer, he flopped around a bit.

Hurriedly, I got down on my hands and knees, unbound him, and took the tape off his mouth.

"Pho!" he exclaimed, before bursting into tears. "Pho, I thought I'd never see you again."

"I'm sorry," I said. "Sorry that you got into trouble like this."

He clung to my neck for a long time, eventually letting me go when his tears had run their course.

"How did you find me?" he asked.

"Brother Pabhassaro led me here."

"He's the one who brought me down here," Jak said. "How are we going to get out?"

I admitted that I did not know. I used the torch to search the room. Aside from the doorway by which I had entered, there were no others. No windows, certainly. If we were going to get out, it was going to be through the door. I got up, examined it, tested its strength. It opened inwards, which would make it harder to pry open. Aside from that it was a solid piece of wood and nothing less than an ax was going to make any difference to it. And of course, there was no ax lying about for convenient use.

"Can you get out?" Jak asked.

I shook my head.

"What are we going to do, Pho?"

"I don't know."

"Did you bring the mobile phone?"

I had. I dug in my bag, excited. But when I tried to call out, I couldn't get a signal.

"It won't work down here," I said.

He took the phone, examined it, a look of frustration passing across the features of his face. "We can't get a signal."

I eventually sat down next to him, turned the light off.

"Can't you leave the light on?" Jak asked. He was dejected in a big way.

"We need to save the light," I said. "I need to think for a minute."

"We're not going to get out of here, are we?"

"Just let me think."

"Pho, I don't want to die in here!"

"We're not going to," I said forcefully, "just give me some time to think."

He lapsed into silence.

Brother Pabhassaro—how could I have been so stupid? Of course he was the one who had killed Sister Moi and Brother Pandito. He had convenient access to the Garden and its secrets, he had the tools needed to do the job—hammers to hit people on the back of the head, ropes to string them up, chains to choke them with. And he must be in league with Chao, in one fashion or another. What sort of coincidence was that?

I had been so sure, though, so sure that the killer was someone else. How could I have been so completely mistaken? And now my mistake might cost Jak and myself our lives. How stupid could I be?

Pabhassaro, Pabhassaro, Pabhassaro . . . why hadn't it occurred to me? Of course he would be working hand in hand with the abbot. No doubt the abbot had paid him handsomely for his services. No doubt Pabhassaro was the one who had hit me over the head that night at the rubbish heap. He could come and go and no one would be the wiser.

How could I have miscalculated so badly?

A more defensive part of my psyche argued that I was a Buddhist monk, not a police officer and certainly not a homicide detective. It had been many years since I had worn the uniform of a police officer, and even then, I had been on the narcotics squad and had seen little in the way of dead bodies and murder, although what I had seen had been enough to last me a lifetime.

"What are we going to do, Pho?"

Jak's voice sounded forlorn in the darkness. There was more than a hint of fear to it.

"Just let me think," I said, trying to soothe him.

It was a pertinent question: What were we going to do?

At that moment, I didn't have a clue.

THREE

"Let's get some rest," I suggested. I needed it. My head was throbbing, my nose was throbbing, my gut was wound up tight making thought all but impossible. "Let's just lie down here and get some rest, okay?"

We did the best we could, lying there on the cold concrete floor, to make ourselves comfortable. Jak laid right next to me, holding my arm with his hand as if afraid we might somehow be separated again while we slept.

Surprisingly enough, I managed to fall asleep.

In the morning—was it morning? I had no way of knowing—I found Jak fast asleep beside me. I sat up, moaned as my various aches and pains protested. At least my head felt somewhat clearer. I used the torch to search the room again, hoping to see something that I had missed the night before. There was nothing.

I needed to go to the bathroom, was going to have to pick a corner and use it though my sensibilities rebelled.

Afterward, I sat down next to Jak and watched him as he slept. I didn't have the heart to wake him up. Reality, at that moment, wasn't as nice as a good dream—or at least unconsciousness, as the case may be. At least he had not come to harm . . . at least not yet. And if I had anything to say about it, we were going to get out of this room and see the light of day and sooner rather than later.

I searched the room again, this time paying particular attention to its construction. Firstly, it had a wooden roof, composed of solid-looking two-by-eights, held together by two-by-four crossbeams. The walls of the room were also composed of two-by-eights, but these spaced out every two feet or so, leaving gaps. The gaps were bare earth. If we had something to dig with, we could try creating a new tunnel, but we had nothing to use so that idea was pointless.

The door was solid. I pulled on the handle and it budged not so much as a centimeter. I tried ramming my shoulder into it and the only thing I managed to accomplish was to wake Jak.

"Pho?"

"Trying to find a way out of here," I said.

"What's that smell?"

"I had to pee."

"So do I."

I showed him the "pee corner" and he went about his business as I continued to examine the door, trying to find some weakness in it that I could exploit. But there were none.

It was frustrating. This whole case had been one dead end after another and finally, when things had started to roll, I managed to get myself locked up with no way out. Lady Luck certainly wasn't with me, not this time around.

"Pho, what are we going to do if we can't get out of here?"

"I don't know," I said. That was the truth. I had no idea. Aside from saying that we were most likely going to die, what else could I say?

"Pho, I'm scared."

"So am I."

"I mean it, Pho. I'm really scared. I don't want to die!"

"We're not going to die," I said as soothingly as I could.

"Yes we are."

"We have to remain positive—we're going to find a way out. Just hang on."

"Pho, I'm hungry."

"If you find something to eat, have at it."

"Really, I'm starving."

"What do you want me to do about it?" I demanded, starting to lose my temper. It didn't take a whole lot to set me off, not me and my temper. That was my biggest fault and failing: I got angry at the drop of a dime. Always had, probably always would, no matter how much I worked on it.

"I'm hungry, Pho," he said, his voice quiet, filled with grief. "I don't want to die in here."

"We're not going to die in here," I said. I tried to sound convincing. "I have an idea."

"You do? What is it?"

"I need to think about it for a minute." Truth was, I didn't have an idea, but I wanted to say something to comfort him, even if it was a small fib. The last thing I needed was for him to panic. Panicking wasn't going to help either one of us.

Then I did have an idea. I went to the far corner of the room opposite the door and looked carefully at the two-by-eights holding up the ceiling. They were ancient, must have been in use for sixty years or more. The bottoms were crumbly and I wondered what would happen if I shook a few loose. Would the ceiling collapse? Would it be like a house of cards—would disturbing one of the cards at the bottom be enough to bring part of the ceiling down? And if it did, would we be able to dig out way up to the surface?

"Come here," I said.

Jak came to stand by my side.

"If we can displace one of these boards, I think we might be able to get out of here."

He examined the boards for himself, craned his neck to look up at the ceiling, which the two-by-eights were holding up.

"I'm not sure that's a good idea," he said.

"It's the only idea I have. What about you?"

He pursed his lips, frowned.

"What if the whole thing comes down?" he asked.

"That's a risk we'll have to take," I replied. I didn't think it was likely but there was no way to be sure.

I pulled at the board in front of me. It would not move. The weight of the ceiling was pressing down on it, pushing it flush with the concrete floor. I tried several other boards, with the same results.

"We need to dig into the dirt, get behind the boards, get some leverage," I said. I scratched at the hard earth with my fingers.

"Do you have something in your bag we can use?" Jak asked.

Did I? If fact I did: I had a book on dharma that I had been intending to read. It had a hardback cover. Though I hated to abuse the book in that fashion, there was no choice. I ripped the front cover off, then the back, handing one to Jak, using the other myself. We got on opposite sides of a two-by-eight and went to work.

It was slow going. Extremely slow going. And in the damp, close atmosphere of the room we were soon sweating and thirsty. After about an hour, though, we had made some progress.

I used my outermost robe to slide behind the two-by-eight so that Jak and I could get on either end of the robe and give it a good pull. If we were lucky—and luck had been hard to come by thus far—we would be able to dislodge the board.

We gave it a shot. Jak pulled for all he was worth. I did likewise. But the board wasn't about to give. That's when I realized that we would have better luck trying to pry it loose from closer to the floor, rather than in the middle. So we spent another hour, on our knees, carving out enough earth to get the robe through it so that we could try again.

"I think it's going to work this time," Jak said hopefully.

I hoped so. Our torch was dying and soon we would be reduced to complete darkness. We got the robe positioned, grabbed our respective ends, pulled for all we were worth.

Success!

The board slid forward suddenly and a hail of dust and dirt fell on our heads. But no more than that. We were going to have to dislodge several boards if we wanted to bring the ceiling down.

"Now what are we going to do?" Jak asked, because the book covers were quickly becoming useless and we had nothing else to dig with.

I sat down on the floor, sighed, fought to catch my breath. All the work had made my head start aching again. I might be good for another board or two, but that was going to be all. And I doubted whether our torchlight would last long enough for the removal of even one board, much less several.

"I need to take a rest," I said. I had turned the torch off and we sat in the dark. I could hear Jak's breathing, the swish of his robes as he moved, his own sigh of resignation.

A wave of defeat washed through me and I waved my head back and forth in silent, unseen protest.

FOUR

We had sat in silence for perhaps an hour, resting, resigning ourselves to our fate. Then, suddenly, I heard the trap door to the tunnel open and footsteps echo down the hall.

"Quiet," I whispered. "Someone's coming."

The door opened from the left, so Jak and I got on the right so that whoever was coming wouldn't see us, not at first.

The footsteps were heavy, assured, undoubtedly those of Brother Pabhassaro. Was he bringing food? Was he going to let us go? Had he come to finish us off?

The footsteps stopped just outside the door.

"Ananda?"

It was Pabhassaro's voice.

"Ananda, I know you're in there. I know you can hear me."

I remained silent, urged Jak to be absolutely silent as well.

"Come on, Ananda, let's not play games. I've brought some food. Just move away from the door and I'll bring it in. No funny stuff, Ananda. You don't want to make me mad."

I remained silent.

He knocked on the door.

I jumped, was startled, though I should not have been.

"Ananda?"

His voice sounded uncertain.

"You asleep?"

Silence.

"I'm coming in."

I heard the handle to the door rattle, and sure enough the door started to open. When it was about halfway open I threw all my weight into it and banged it shut as hard as I could, hoping to knock Pabhassaro off his feet.

I did.

I dragged the door open, flipped on the torch, urged Jak to make a run for it. Jak, despite the hitch in his step, bounded over

Pabhassaro and rushed down the passageway. I scampered after him, but Pabhassaro caught my leg as I tried to rush past. He did more than catch my leg: He caught hold of my calf, the very same calf that had been raked by the crocodile's claws.

I collapsed in agony on top of him, pain screaming up my leg into my belly.

His fingers continued to dig into the flesh of my calf and he was trying to right himself, to get to his feet. Frightened half out of my mind, I let my feet fly, caught him in the chest with one foot, heaved him backwards. It was enough to get him to release his grip. I scrambled to my feet, but he caught hold of my ankle and downed me again.

I shouted for help, no longer much aware of what I was doing. All I could think of was that I needed to escape from Pabhassaro and get out of that cellar before he left me down there to die of starvation and dehydration.

In the darkness and shadow it was hard to see clearly. I kicked with my feet—wildly, blindly, more from nerves than any plan of action. One of my kicks caught Pabhassaro in the throat and forced him backward. His head hit the solid wood of the door and he went down with a groan.

Scrambling to my feet, I dashed down the passageway after Jak and rushed up the ladder and to freedom.

CHAPTER EIGHT

"It is not stability that you need, it is balance."
—*The Sage's Tao Te Ching: A New Interpretation, #77*

ONE

"Help me with this ladder!" I shouted.

Jak grabbed one side, I grabbed the other and we lifted it. We could hear Pabhassaro's footsteps down in the tunnel, coming closer. We yanked on the ladder, trying to get it up and out of the tunnel as quickly as possible. We were rewarded with the sight of Pabhassaro down below, snarling at us, shouting and furious—but unable to get out.

After we had thrown the ladder to one side, I paused to catch my breath and calm my racing nerves. I was reminded once again that I was on the other side of fifty and not getting any younger. Jak looked scared out of his mind and ran off, his hips pumping up and down furiously as he ran. I hoped he had enough presence of mind to sound the alarm and get some help.

I pushed on the bear exhibit, got the top of the tunnel sealed. Then I stood there, by the exhibit, trying to catch my breath.

A group of tourists passed by while making the circuit of the Garden. They paused to give me curious looks. Whether they could hear Pabhassaro shouting curses from below, I did not know.

From the position of the sun, I guessed it was mid-morning or thereabouts. After a night spent down in that hole, the fresh breeze was wonderful and relaxing—never had air smelled so clean, so desirous, so good on the skin.

Jak eventually returned with about twenty monks trailing behind him. He wasn't taking any chances.

Kusalo hurried to greet me. "Father Ananda? What on earth happened?"

I explained as quickly as I could.

"So Pabhassaro is the killer?" Kusalo asked.

"It looks that way," I said.

"We need to get you cleaned up," Kusalo said, giving me a once-over with his eyes.

"My head is pounding," I admitted. "I could use some aspirin."

He led Jak and myself away while the other monks congregated around the bear exhibit, waiting for the police to show up and arrest Brother Pabhassaro.

Back in the dorm room, I lay on my mat gratefully, not realizing how exhausted I was, how tired, how my limbs were on fire with various aches and agonies.

Brother Kusalo offered aspirin, water. I gulped down two aspirin, laid my head back, sighed. He poked and prodded at my various bandages, made unhappy faces, got out a med kit and got to work. While he did this, I asked what was happening.

"The abbot was taken into custody," he said.

That much I knew. "What else?"

"Well, the abbot says he's innocent, has no idea what's going on. Like anyone believes him. Also, the children in that lorry were found and turned over to Immigration officials—the story has been in all the newspapers. The prime minister himself has been commenting on it—he wants the culprits found and prosecuted."

"If not beheaded," I said.

"That's one way of putting it," Kusalo agreed. "Of course, we're all embarrassed—we had no idea what was going on. I thought we were running a legitimate program. I had no idea that these kids were being trafficked. The thought never occurred to me. I mean, come on, this is a monastery. But if you read the newspapers, you'd think we were all involved in the mafia and happy participants at that."

Monks, as Jenjira had wisely pointed out, got up to the most unholy of things.

"You've been in the paper, too," Kusalo added. "You and your novice. You went missing and there's been all sorts of speculation as to what happened to you. The television stations have been showing your picture constantly."

Someone noticed. For that, I was grateful.

"And a certain friend of ours is in hot water—really hot water. *Thai Rath* ran pictures of Mr. A surveying his poppy fields. The prime minister has been commenting on that case too, vowing that justice will be done and all that."

"I sure hope so," I said.

"Anyway, Immigration is sorting out the mess with the children. They took all our records—they're trying to get to the bottom of things."

"Your monastery was just a stop on the way," I said.

"Apparently."

He had finished with the bandaging on my leg and was now sitting close to me, ready to peel the bandages off my nose and redo them.

"Do you have to?" I asked.

"Yes," he replied firmly. "You don't want this to become infected—then you'll really be up a creek without a paddle."

I'd had enough pain for one day and did not want any more. In fact, I wanted to sleep for a long, long time and not be bothered by anyone. But such was not to be.

Gingerly, being as careful as he could, Kusalo peeled away the bandages from my face.

"That looks pretty," he said, surveying my broken nose.

"Just hurry up," I said.

He hurried, taping my nose up as best he could. There wasn't much else to be done with a broken nose except keep it in its proper position until it heals properly. Most of the nose is cartilage and nothing more.

After he had done that, he surveyed the back of my head, offered some *tsk tsks* of disapproval, as if it was my fault that I had been beaten by someone or other. Then he checked over the rest of my body to make sure that nothing else was broken or in disrepair. After all of this he began to work on Jak, checking him out, urging him to take some aspirin and lie down.

"Well, you said you wanted to shake things up," Kusalo said. "You succeeded. Once Pabhassaro's out of the way, things ought to quiet down—at least I hope they do."

I wasn't so sure of that, but I remained silent.

TWO

For the remainder of the day I rested, refusing all requests from the media for an interview and picture. Mostly I slept. My head continued to throb and pound and I thought it would never stop, but after several aspirins it finally quieted.

The third day of mourning for Brother Pandito had been that day. Now it was time for his cremation. In the late afternoon I heard the mourners as they carried Pandito's coffin around the crematorium three times. I heard the loud buzzer sound that signals one and all that the crematorium is about to be turned on—that was the signal to get clear. Some monks like to lie inside the crematorium itself to meditate on death. If the alarm goes off, it's time to move on unless one wants to experience death firsthand.

Eventually I heard the crematorium itself come on, burning Pandito and his coffin, leaving little behind but a few bones and a pile of ashes.

Still I continued to rest, sleeping when I could, or just lying with my eyes closed and my body at rest.

Jak slept soundly the entire day, which did not surprise me in the slightest. He'd been through a lot.

In the evening, after the funeral ceremony was over, the parking lot began to clear out. Brother Kusalo came to the dorm room to inform me that Jenjira wanted to talk to me. I got up, went to the door, ushered her inside before any of the other reporters could see me.

"Father Ananda, I'm so relieved," she said straightaway.

"Thanks."

"What happened?"

I explained.

"Do you think this Pabhassaro guy is the one who killed the brother and sister?"

I shook my head. No, that was not what I thought at all.

"Then who?" she asked.

"That's what we're going to find out," I said. "And I'm going to need your help."

Then I smiled.

THREE

I was in a bit of a pickle. I knew who the murderer was, but how to prove it? I needed a confession, a confirmation of my suspicions. I needed the killer to explain what he had done and why. I needed his help, his cooperation. Getting it was going to prove difficult.

I got up, left Jak in the care of the other novices, and went outside. It was early evening. Numerous people still milled about, mostly reporters and media types. The light was fading and there was no time like the present to get the deed over and done with. Jenjira and her entourage were close by; she gave me a thumbs up. Now or never. She and her team were prepared and ready for action.

I found Brother Kusalo in the funeral hall and asked him if I might have another look through the monastery's files. He made little effort to hide his exasperation with me and my ways, but nevertheless he agreed.

"I promise this will be the last time," I said, trying to cheer him up.

"That's okay," he replied. "I've got to clean up the abbot's office anyway, get prepared for a new abbot—we're not sure who that's going to be yet."

"I'm sure everything will get back to normal soon," I replied.

"I hope so."

So did I. If only so that I could pack my bag and get out of this murderous monastery and be on my way.

In the office, Kusalo flipped on the lights, nodded his head in the direction of the files, inviting me to have a look while he took a seat at his desk. Instead of looking through the files, though, I stood on the other side of his desk and gave him a long, searching look.

"What?" he asked.

"There's a file in there for everyone in this place except you," I said quietly.

He remained silent. His somewhat cheerful demeanor became sour. He began twisting his hands together nervously.

"Can you explain that?" I asked.

"I'm sure it's just an oversight," he replied, frowning. "I filled out the application form just like everybody else. You must have just missed it."

"I didn't miss it," I said. "I searched from start to finish and there's no file in there with your name on it."

He looked uncomfortable. That made me glad. I was also glad to have the desk between us. I was not sure about Kusalo. He did not look that strong, but he was much younger than I was, much more mobile, and probably a damn sight better in a fight.

"Well, it's just a mistake, then," Kusalo said, shrugging, trying to dismiss the matter.

"I'm not so sure of that," I replied. "Would you care to give me a sample of your handwriting?"

"What for?"

"So that I can compare it to the note that was found on Sister Moi, the note that enticed her out to the Garden on the night she was killed. You remember?"

"You think I wrote that note?"

"I'm almost sure of it," I said. "I'd be willing to bet a whole lot of money on it. And I think you wrote the note to Brother Pandito too."

"Father Ananda, this is ridiculous. I didn't have anything to do with any of this."

"Are you quite sure about that?" I asked.

Silence fell.

I saw his eyes darting to the bottle of chili powder that he kept on his desk in the midst of all the clutter.

"That's how you did it, isn't it?" I asked.

"Excuse me?"

"The chili powder—you blinded them first by throwing chili powder in their eyes. That's why they had those red flakes on their faces. After that you were pretty much free to do what you pleased, weren't you? They would be incapacitated, unable to protect themselves. Probably couldn't even see what was going on. That's how you did it, isn't it? Really rather clever."

He remained silent, his eyes darting to the bottle again as if to judge how fast he could grab it and likewise put me out of commission. I was prepared for that, if that's what it took. Actually I was hoping he would go for it—that would be proof that he knew what I was talking about, that he was guilty.

"I just want to know why," I said. "Can you tell me that? A pregnant nun—how could you do such a thing?"

"How was I supposed to know she was pregnant?"

I dug around in my monk's bag, produced letters that I had stolen from Kusalo's kuti. He eyed them, paled. His fingers began to shake. The letters were the ones from Panya to Moi, the ones in which he pleaded with her to leave the monastery with him and start a family.

"You know what these are, don't you?" I said. "I found them in your *kuti*. I found a lot of other things in your *kuti* too, for that matter. You sure do have a lot of secrets. Not to mention a fat bank account."

"You had no right to be going through my personal belongings!"

"That's where you're wrong," I said. "As a representative of the Maha Thera Samakhom, I can pretty much do as I please. You're a monk, after all—or are you? Is that just a sham too?"

"What are you talking about?"

"You're a liar," I said easily. "You've been lying to me since the day I got here. You've been casting suspicion on other people, like Brother Pabhassaro, trying to confuse me."

"I have not."

"You can quit pretending now. I don't buy it. It was you that night out at the rubbish heap—you're the one who hit me over the head and took that letter that I'd found, not Brother Silapalo. It was you."

"It was not!"

"I found that letter in your kuti—I remember that it was addressed to the abbot and had coffee stains on it. How do you explain that? How did you come into possession of that letter unless you took it from my pocket while I was unconscious?"

I now produced this letter so that he could see that I was telling the truth.

"Isn't it funny that this letter is from Sister Mettha and was addressed to the abbot—she was suspicious about your repatriation program, didn't trust you, so she wrote to the abbot himself, hoping to bypass you. But she didn't succeed, did she?

How many other things did you intercept before the abbot had a chance to look at them?"

"You can't prove anything."

"That's where you're wrong, Kusalo. I can keep digging in this bag and produce all sorts of stuff. Shall I continue? Shall we check your robes and see if you have a patch missing. You do, don't you? In fact, I already checked your spare robes in your *kuti*—your repair job was rather sloppy, I must say."

He said nothing.

"Why?" I asked. "I want to understand why."

"They were threatening the repatriation program. Do you know how much money we've been receiving to process these kids? Is that what you want, Father Ananda—a cut of the profits? A nice fat sum to put in your own bank account? Is that it—you're jealous?"

"The abbot was clueless, wasn't he?" I asked.

Kusalo snorted. "The abbot is a buffalo. He wouldn't be able to find his butt if he didn't have to sit on it every day."

"And you're the one who started this program, aren't you? It was your idea."

"Of course it was. Do you know how much money they offered me?"

"You're a monk. What do you care about money?"

He laughed. Then, with a swiftness that surprised me, he had the bottle of chili powder in his hands, the top off, and was tossing it in the direction of my face.

I turned away immediately but still caught some on my nose and lips and instantly began sneezing.

He got up from the desk, bounded around it in my direction, a chain in his hands.

I hollered for help, but my plea was quickly cut off. Kusalo, behind me, began to choke me with the chain. I struggled against it feebly, feeling pain explode in various parts of my body. The chain bit into my neck, cutting off my oxygen. I clutched at it futilely. He was much too strong for me. I tried to shout, could do nothing more than gasp.

Then the door to the office burst open and Jenjira and her entourage, along with Lt Poom and officials from the Immigration Department, poured into the room.

Kusalo was quickly forced to the ground, handcuffed, taken away.

I rubbed at my throat, hoping that no serious damage had been done. I was surprised at Kusalo's quickness—I hadn't expected him to be so fast.

"Father Ananda, are you alright?" Jenjira asked, peering up at me and squinting, her face full of concern.

"I'm fine," I said. Or rather squawked. "I need to sit down."

She got a chair and I sat, breathing heavily, frightened out of my wits. My heart was pounding in my chest. Every throb of blood through my body made the back of my head seize up in agony. But at least it was all over now. Finally.

"Have some water," Jenjira said, handing me a plastic bottle of water.

I accepted it gratefully. "Did you get it all on tape?" I asked her, digging into my robe pockets and fetching her transmitter.

"Certainly did, Father. We're going to fry his ass. Pardon my language."

"The police need to search his *kuti*—he's got a lot of stuff in there."

"Don't you worry about that now," she said. "You've done enough for one day."

FOUR

"How did you know it was Kusalo?" Jak asked later that evening as we prepared for bed.

"He was the only one who fit all the facts," I said.

"I don't understand."

"He was the one who found me that night out by the rubbish heap—he found me because he was the one who hit me. No one else was up and around that night. Only him."

"And?"

"Well, when I searched through the files, I was waiting to find his file so that I could check his handwriting. I was worried about it—I didn't want him to think that I suspected him. I needed his cooperation and help. I went through all the files myself, and there was no file for him. He must have removed it, afraid that I was going to see it. He was afraid I was going to recognize his handwriting. But at the time I thought it was just an oversight."

"And?"

"Well, one thing led to another. He was the one who told me about Brother Panya and Sister Moi. He was the one who tried to cast suspicion on Brother Pabhassaro."

"But Pabhassaro was in on it."

"He was, yes, but only as an accomplice. They were both working for Mr. A. Kusalo was the leader. Pabhassaro was just a flunky."

"So what's going to happen to them now?"

"They'll be charged with the murders of Sister Moi and Brother Pandito. We've got enough evidence to make sure the charges stick."

"So can we go home now?"

"If that's what you want. But I was thinking we would go north, go pay respects to your mother."

His eyes brightened. Then he rewarded me with a beaming smile.

FIVE

We spent the night at Wat Yai, in the huge dorm, right in the center—Jak was still paranoid about harm coming to us.

In the morning we made the alms round with a monk named Dhammanando and several *dek wat*. I was in no condition to be making an alms round, yet I could not resist the chance for a stroll in the countryside. It made all my aches and pains feel better somehow. It calmed my over-anxious mind.

Representatives from the Maha Thera Samakhom showed up during breakfast to assess the situation at Wat Yai and attempt a bit of damage control. I gave them the letters that Panya had written to Sister Moi after verifying that Panya had indeed written them. Panya was no longer a monk; the representatives planned to defrock him that morning. To engage in sexual activity would mean instant "defeat" for a Buddhist monk. By the very act itself, a monk lost his monkhood though he could continue to wear the robes and pretend he had not.

His brother Subha would also be defrocked for lying. In Buddhism, there are five basic precepts that everyone must keep: Not to kill, not to steal, not to lie, not to engage in sexual misbehavior and not to gamble. For a monk to break one of these very basic fundamental precepts was grounds for defrocking.

Jak was anxious to leave and so was I. But there was one small detail I wanted to clear up before our departure. After breakfast, I found Brother Silapalo in the breakfast hall and took him to one side.

"When I interviewed you," I said, "it was clear to me that you knew something, or had done something, that you were guilty of something. Am I right?"

He licked his lips, frowned, offered a despairing look.

"What was it?" I pressed.

"I saw Pabhassaro and Kusalo with Pandito that night . . . that night when Pandito was killed. I didn't want to say anything. People who speak up . . . well, they get murdered around here."

That was certainly true.

"So you were afraid?" I asked.

"I'm sorry. I should have told you. But I was afraid of what would happen to me."

I told him to never mind, that it was okay, that I understood. And I did. Our mafia types act with impunity—the orange robes of a monk notwithstanding. I could understand his fear because I had once shared it, had once gone along with the status quo like everyone else. Perhaps when Silapalo got older, he might begin to see things differently.

"Next time," I said, "and if there is a next time, trust me, okay?"

He said that he would.

SIX

Jak and I spent several days more at Wat Yai, resting, recovering. On a Friday we took our leave, saying goodbye to the monks and nuns, and soon found ourselves on a bus headed north—a bus packed with bodies.

"Pho, you're not mad at me, are you?" Jak asked, as our journey to his hometown got underway.

"Why would I be mad at you?"

"For what I said . . . the other day . . . you know."

I knew. His talk of suicide.

"No, I'm not mad at you. Whenever you feel bad like that, you can talk to me and I'll try to help you. But suicide isn't the answer to the problem."

"I know."

"Jak, you're going to find that lots of people have disabilities, and they all feel the same way you do—they don't like being stared out, being singled out, being made fun of. But those things—that's not your problem. If people want to be stupid, what can you do? You just have to live your life and ignore those people. Don't let them get to you."

"I know."

"And you also know that many people with disabilities enjoy their lives, enjoy living. They work, go to school, have families—you don't need to let your disability get in the way of anything you want to do in your life. You hear me?"

"I know."

"I know you know. I'm just reminding you."

He was silent. He stared out the window at the passing countryside. The bus hurtled down the country side as if fleeing the scene of some crime.

"Pho?"

"Yes?"

"I'm hungry."